The Clover Chronicles

Battling Brelyn

Mya Kay

The TMG Firm

New York

The TMG Firm, LLC
112 W. 34th Street
17th and 18th Floors
New York, NY 10120
www.thetmgfirm.com

The Clover Chronicles: Battling Brelyn
Copyright © 2016 Mya K. Douglas
Published and edited by The TMG Firm, LLC

For more information about special discounts for bulk purchase, please contact The TMG Firm at 1-888-984-3864 ext 12 or publishing@thetmgfirm.com

ISBN: 978-0-99835-658-7
Library of Congress Control Number: 2016963022
All rights reserved

First The TMG Firm Trade Paperback Edition April 2017
Printed in the United States of America

Cover created and designed by Murphy Rae Hopkins
for Indie Solutions.

FOREWORD

Incredible Woman

My, oh, my...Mya, what an incredible woman. Ever since Mya was young in age and little in size everyone around her knew she had infinite potential. As a kid, Mya was very sensitive, and very emotional. I guess that's why she's able to put so much emotion into the stories she writes, even when touching on sensitive subjects. She's always been very intelligent, very creative, very determined and very passionate about the people she loves. That's why so many people love her, not just for her accomplishments, but love her for being so genuine.

Mya and I were raised in the same neighborhood during the same years. We were both faced with the same harsh conditions growing up in a very poor neighborhood presented. Just like me, she was able to surpass levels doubters didn't expect her to reach. She even took it a step further than most who believed in her thought was possible. She's a believer, an overachiever, and an overall incredible woman. Mya has a God-given talent, fused with an incredible work ethic, so the sky's not the limit for her; it's just the starting point! Soaring to unimaginable heights will be Mya's testimony. A testimony that will influence others to soar higher than they ever imagined.

Mya is not just a phenomenal author, she has a great soul and comes from a great family. She's a great friend and an all-around beautiful person who is greatly appreciated by everyone around her. Hard work and dedication are mandatory requirements if you expect to be successful. It would be difficult to find a person whose more dedicated and applies themselves more than she does.

She has a good heart, she's in good health and she's extremely good at what she does. A black woman telling stories with a writing technique that will change the world. I predict nothing but good things to happen for her in the future. She's a modern day Maya Angelou...an incredible woman!

—Barry "Cassidy" Reese
  Platinum Selling Recording Artist

ACKNOWLEDGMENTS

My all belongs to Christ. I never could've imagined that He could do what He's done in my life. What a beautiful mess I was. Thank you Lord for giving me the gift of salvation. For that, I owe You everything. I'll give my always to You.

SD Green and The TMG Firm: You laid an amazing foundation for authors to get their voices heard. Thanks for believing in my work, for giving me a chance to spread my wings with two celebrity collaborations and for embracing me from day one. Looking forward to being with the firm for many years to come.

I'll always love my momma. She's my favorite girl! Momma Linda, you sacrificed it all just so I could dream. If I'm just a fraction of the woman you are, I'll be forever grateful. It's time for you to live an Ephesians 3:20 life. Thanks for being my best friend. I love you endlessly.

Malik Douglas: My brother, my protector, my best friend, my ace. I love you to pieces. Big brothers rule the world! Thanks for your support and your love. It pushes me on my hardest of days.

To the readers: Wow. My ninth published novel! Thanks for believing in me and for trusting my pen game. I hope you enjoy the Clover family. Love you all!

Chapter 1

It all started when I went to open my toothpaste. My finger locked and I couldn't get it open. I could easily lift 125 pounds at our home gym, but that morning, I couldn't open my toothpaste. When I finally got it open, it took me even longer to put the toothpaste on the toothbrush. The whole process took thirty minutes, and I hadn't even started brushing my teeth. As soon as I put the brush in my mouth and moved it back and forth, my gums began to bleed. I immediately knew something was wrong.

I dropped my toothbrush, tried to return to my bedroom and fell to the floor. My knees and legs, in fact, my entire body, throbbed. I could no longer walk through my door; I could only crawl. Thank God, I hadn't closed the door all of the way. I knew the doorknob would've given me a hard time.

"Daddy!" I screamed. I was now crying and even the simple act of breathing hurt. If there was ever a time I hated our 7,500 square foot home, it was this day. The sheer size of the house required me to yell, and my chest was killing me. "Dad, Mom....I need you..." I then saw Desmond, my older brother. He threw his iPad to the ground and ran to my aid.

"Bre, what's wrong?" he asked.

I cried and held his hand while covering my face with my free hand. I hated being weak. It's not what we, the Clovers, were made of. Through the small spaces between my fingers, I saw my parents running down the hallway. My dad was going full speed. I smirked internally thinking about all the track trophies he'd won back in his high school days.

"Baby girl, what is it?" He swooped me into his arms in one, fast motion. At that point, Emé and Cashmere, my older sisters, were now standing beside my crying mother. In less than two minutes, we were all in the family SUV and our driver, Tony, was speeding towards the hospital. I saw Desmond secure the house with one push of his phone; such conveniences made me thankful that we were billionaires.

Chestnut Hill Hospital's emergency room was packed by the time we arrived. I screamed in agony the entire drive while my mother quietly prayed and my father gently rubbed my stomach. "God, take me before you take my baby," my mother whispered repeatedly. Something deep inside told me that this was one problem my daddy's billions would not be able to fix and I was right.

Eventually, I was diagnosed with lupus. It was a milder form, but it was nonetheless lupus. Today marked five months since my diagnosis, and we were sitting at the hospital because I had another attack. That's pretty much how things flowed – an attack here, an attack there, lots of pills, including prednisone. The worst part of it all – not being able to be as active as I used to be. But I was thankful that I wasn't on dialysis. Due to my overall healthy lifestyle, my kidneys were strong. I prayed every day that they remained that way and wouldn't fail.

Desmond and Cashmere prayed with me every day before we left for school. It was refreshing to have a strong, spiritual unit inside my family. As I sat in the hospital bed, Desmond read to me from a chapter of the book of Psalms. He looked up and winked, then kissed me on my forehead.

"I love you, Bre," he said.

"I love you more, Des," I answered, smiling weakly. The drugs were taking effect. My parents stood on the other side of my door discussing my illness with my doctors. I had the strongest medical team ever and still, the disease remained. When Desmond walked outside to talk to my parents, I closed my eyes and prayed "God, I love you so much. I just want to live and have a couple of forevers with my family. Can you make that possible? Please. I promise to serve you with my life. Amen."

I wiped a lone tear from my eye as I drifted off to sleep.

❀ ❀ ❀

"Papa, that's not fair," I whined, turning to Mom for help. I had been home from the hospital for a few days now. She pursed her lips and shook her head. The bomb Dad dropped on me was worse than the one that we'd just received from the doctor. Bodies by Brelyn, my fitness company, had been my focus for the past year. Starting my own business came naturally to me being that my family bred entrepreneurs, but it wasn't until I came upon an online brochure that I realized I could start fitness classes. Bodies by Brelyn perfectly suited my personality, and it would eventually allow me to work my up to building my own gym. Now, I sat here listening to my parents and siblings kill any thought behind that dream.

"It's just temporary, Bre," Cashmere said.

"Easy for you to say. You'll still make your shirts," I huffed.

Cashmere's eyes widened at my comment. I knew I was being difficult, but my name had been tarnished. Without a business, would I even fit in with the rest of my family?

"It's my life. I love teaching classes. I wanted to have a grand opening this summer," I continued to whine. "Why do I have to give up everything?"

Tears sprang to my eyes, and I let them fall. Since being diagnosed with lupus, I had pretty much been on a restricted diet, unable to eat most of the things I loved and unable to do much without assistance, especially when I had an attack. The three classes I taught were aerobics and a cycling class that grew from three members to over thirty in just under a few months. Each of my classes was an hour long, and I ran about six sessions a week, mostly on Saturdays. My father and I worked on the business plan most of the last year, and I was excited to follow in his footsteps.

After school, I would train a group of about thirty faithful Bodies by Brelyn members. Some were obese teens who were given strict instructions to lose weight, while others were college students and athletes. I even trained a few adults. I loved everything about helping them shape their bodies and reach their individual desired body goals. Things had been going well when I was first diagnosed with lupus. The doctor said it may actually be good for me to continue training my clients. But last week after a trip to the hospital, I collapsed during a cycling class; which unfortunately for me my dad just so happened to have been taking.

"He said light cardio and light training," my mom chimed in, breaking into my thoughts, "you exert yourself more than you should when you train others. Honey, you have to take it easy. I know you hate giving up so much of yourself, but..."

"This is stupid," I huffed, sitting on the couch as Cashmere tried to console me. "This sucks."

"I have typed up a letter that I think you should send to your members," Mom continued, moving to sit next to me. "We'll have a party for everyone and announce a temporary solution for them."

"Whatever," I mumbled, getting up. I didn't care what they did. It didn't seem like I had much of a choice anyway.

"Bre, it's just temporary," Cashmere said for the millionth time.

I stood up and walked to the doorway. I turned back to my family. "The disease or me not training?" Somehow I think they forgot that lupus was something that didn't have a cure.

❦ ❦ ❦

Despite my parents' stern warnings about increased activity, I decided that a game of horse wouldn't hurt.

"Cheater," I yelled out to Desmond. This was the first time I played ball in the past month, and I felt great. We were playing a few rounds of horse. We were in round number four, which was great exercise for me. If it had been last week, I would've gotten to the letter *H* and been done.

"R," Desmond said, ignoring my whining. I jumped up to copy his shot and made it.

"In your face, sucker," I yelled walking past him. I looked over and saw Mama place a water container down. She'd been watching since we started. I had to deal her being over-protective at this point, and there was nothing I could do about it. I think she feared me having another attack and not being able to hear my cries for help.

Thirty minutes later, Mom called us in for dinner. Much like every other day, we each sat at our usual places at the table with one small exception. Dad sat at the head, Desmond usually would typically sit to the left of him, but since I'd been sick he'd given his seat up for me. Now Desmond sat next to me, Mom sat to the right of my father and Cashmere next to Mom. It sounds weird that we all specific seats at the table but it had always been that way. Before Emé moved out on her own, she sat right next to Mom. Papa squeezed my shoulder, and I looked up at him.

"A new doctor is coming over from South Korea. He's a Rheumatologist, and he specializes in lupus. I've added him to the payroll."

I put my fork down, confused. "Payroll?"

Mom, Cashmere and Desmond were all smiling as Dad spoke.

"Yes," Dad continued, grabbing my hand. "It's a lot, going back and forth to the hospital for you. I can't stand to see you in there. We're going to set up a hospital room right here in our home, and he'll be on call, as you need him."

I smiled. "That's great, Papa," I said, jumping up to kiss his cheek. "Thanks so much."

"You're getting some of your weight back sis," Cashmere said. "You look great."

I blew her a kiss, and the room erupted in laughter. That was all the inspiration I needed to begin playfully posing. I was pleased with the recent improvements to my body and had no problem showing it. I stood five foot six and shortly after my lupus diagnosis my weight dropped to a hundred and ten pounds. With a rigorous new diet, I'd managed to increase my weight to a healthy one hundred and thirty pounds. I sat down and relished the moment of laughing and joking with my family. For a second everything seemed normal again; that was until the throbbing in my knee quickly reminded me of my reality. Although it was over almost as fast it began, at least I had the chance to feel like a normal teen again for a minute. I finished my dinner with a smile plastered across my face as fresh tears stung my eyes. I refused to let them drop. There was always hope with a praying family.

As a family, we, the Clovers, were extraordinarily blessed, but beneath it all, we were simply a loving family. Emé Kelli Clover, whose twenty-eight, is my father's child from his first marriage. Her mother, Rita, died from cancer when she was six. Emé's mixed Latina and black heritage was evident to anyone who saw her. She is just as tall as Papa, with a presence as regal as her look. Our parents married when Emé was ten. Two years later, in 1998, Desmond Carter Clover, Jr. was born. Cashmere was born in 1999, and I was born in 2000. I'm the baby, Brelyn Michele Clover. When my father met my mother, she was a top jewelry designer with her own line, Reese C. Jewelry. Her jewelry was in high-end retailers and had been covered by several top fashion magazines. Today, her line is called Reese Pieces.

My father is the CEO and owner of Roger Frances Enterprises, the luxury Wine and Distillery Company. My great, great-grandfather, Roger, started the business in California in the late 1800's. Eight years after he tasted his first self-grown grapes and after several failed attempts, Roger Frances Winery was born. Today, our family's wine and beverages are requested by presidents, celebrities and even overseas dignitaries. My father inherited the company when he was just thirty-five, after the death of my grandfather. Thanks to my father's winery and Reese Pieces, my family was worth several billion dollars.

My father was raised in North Philly and my mother in Brooklyn. She moved to Philadelphia for college and never left. My brother, sisters and I were all born and raised right outside of Chestnut Hill, Philadelphia; in Lafayette Hill to be exact.

After dinner, I sought the refuge of my room. I needed a quiet place, away from it all, to take in the dinnertime conversation and my window seat was just the spot. As the thoughts whipped around my mind, I looked over at the box Cashmere dropped on my bed before we headed downstairs for dinner. Getting up slowly, I grabbed it and sat down. I saw the *Cool Cash* label and knew that it was a new shirt from her t-shirt line. Sighing, I began to rip into the box. Even with a box cutter in hand, it took me fifteen minutes just to pull back and cut through the tape that secured the box. When finally I pulled the t-shirt out, I smiled. It read 'Believe Brelyn.' It was Cashmere's daily affirmation that I had to believe things would get better. I had no idea she was turning it into a t-shirt. I smiled weakly and put it on. The gesture was very sweet, and I sincerely appreciated her thoughtfulness, but the t-shirt was another reminder that each of my siblings' businesses was flourishing while mine was in danger of flatlining.

Desmond had his own line of sneakers called, Bricks. They were a cool, retro type of sneaker. He had released three sneakers in just two years and was breaking all kinds of barriers. An NBA player tweeted about his sneakers at the beginning of the season, and his sales shot through the roof. Emé was a theater actress who just started landing major parts in movies. Before following her acting dreams full-time, she obtained an esthetician license, which is how her Empress Skin Care line was birthed. People often asked us how we did it – being young and running a business. We eat, sleep and dream business. Now with my new health challenges, I wasn't so sure if I wanted to focus on business if it couldn't apply to my passion for fitness.

I instinctively touched my gold, four-leaf clover pendant necklace as I placed the shirt back into the box. I was proud of what my parents had instilled in us and even more proud that my siblings were able to do what they loved. I knew that they would never let me feel down or left out just because I had to pause my business. I'd thought of different ways to be an effective trainer without the physical aspect, but a part of me felt it wasn't enough. Would I ever be able to measure up to bearing the Clover name without a financially solvent business like Desmond's or my sisters? How could I call myself a Clover when my sickness had branded me as a weakling, while my parents and siblings seemed to grow stronger by the day?

Chapter 2

Later that night, as I sat in my window reading a book, I squinted as I noticed that there were lights on in the house next door. Mom told me a new family would be moving in, and the boy would be going to our school, The Business & Arts Academy of Philadelphia; but I didn't expect the new neighbors to arrive so soon. This was the first time I'd seen any action. I looked closer and saw an older man walking in and out of the house. And then I saw *him*. He looked right into my eyes but quickly turned away when he noticed I wouldn't.

His dimple was the first thing I noticed as he talked to the older man, but it didn't take long for me to take in the rest of him. He had a caramel complexion with a low cut. A raggedy t-shirt and a pair of sweats covered his small frame, but my fitness eye noticed a few muscles. Even from my second-floor window, I could see his green eyes. Neither his wheelchair or the fact that I couldn't tell how tall he was, took away from his rugged but handsome features. He leaned over, put a box on his lap and moved a little closer to the front door.

I assumed that he must've been some kind of athlete because of the shirt he was wearing. It had the number seven and the word 'Tigers' across the chest. He rolled his wheelchair over and handed the older man a box as he looked back at me and smirked. I waved. He stared at me for a few seconds but didn't wave back. I couldn't blame him for not being friendly. He was the new kid on the block and starting over wasn't easy. I knew firsthand.

"Brelyn," I heard my mother yell. "Come down here, please."

I placed my bookmark in my book and eased off the seat. I paused for a second before moving. I was getting a little dizzy, and I wanted to make sure I had my balance before I ran downstairs. Up here, I could be as weak as I wanted. Down there, I had to make sure they had no reason to alter my life any more than they already had. I wasn't sure what my mom wanted, but I grabbed a jacket just in case. The light spring air had turned chilly since this morning. Once I reached the bottom of the long, winding staircase, I stopped. I could see them moving toward our house from the bay window next to the front door. I closed my eyes to catch my breath. When I opened them again, I was looking right into those green eyes. His eyes.

"Hey," I said, this time, putting a little smile on my face.

"Hey," he said.

My father stood next to the older guy that had been outside with him earlier.

"Brelyn, this is Luke and his son, Saith," he said as I stepped forward to shake Luke's hand. "Saith will be going to school with you all, but I believe him and Cashmere will be in the same classes."

"Yes, sir," he said, not taking his eyes off me. "I'm a junior. Desmond is the sneaker head, right?"

My mom smiled. "Yep. That's my baby boy. You have a pair of his sneakers?"

I rolled my eyes in the air. Saith squinted at me, and I looked away.

"Dad, where is Desmond?" I asked.

"He went out with your sister, Emé. They'll be back shortly."

Luke and my father went into the dining hall to talk. My mother grabbed my hand and kissed it.

"How do you feel, baby girl?"

I closed my eyes and prayed she wouldn't say anything else. If ever there were an awkward moment to ask me about my health, it was now.

"Good." One word answers usually got her to relax. I looked at Saith again. He didn't seem to notice.

"Well, I'll leave you two kids be. It's the weekend so I won't fuss about bedtime," she said, winking at me. I smiled and winked back at her. Even with her fussy ways and her overbearing demeanor, my mom really was one of my best friends. I zipped up my jacket and turned back to Saith.

"You want to sit outside?"

He didn't say anything. He just turned and rolled toward the door. I didn't budge. He opened our large front door, almost with no effort. Even my father struggled with that door sometimes, but I wasn't impressed. He slowly turned his head towards me.

"You coming?"

I walked to the door and grabbed it. "You first," I said, extending my hand to indicate that I was waiting for him to go through the door. We had a flat surface walkway leading up to our front door. I was amazed at how he maneuvered his wheelchair with ease. The sound of the wheels swishing against his hand resonated against the crisp night air. It was still nice out, but I could feel the air through my jacket.

"You excited about school?" I asked, breaking the silence between us.

"No. I don't know anyone," he said. Even with his deep voice, I could hear a bit of nervousness.

"Well, neither did we when we first arrived."

He looked at me and chuckled. "Smarty pants."

"Takes one to know one."

"How you figure?"

"I waved at you earlier, and you didn't even wave back. Were you being smart?"

"No, no. I was just...I thought you were staring at the wheelchair. I hate that."

I got quiet. I loathed pity just as much.

"Nope. I was just being friendly. I've seen worse. Trust me."

He pushed his chair back and forth. Then, he rolled over to the fountain.

"Sit. Your mother will kill me for having you stand while we're out here talking. Come on."

I winced slightly as I silently wondered if my mother had shared my health issues with him. Hoping that she hadn't, I walked behind him and sat down on the fountain's edge. I kept staring at him, but not because of the chair. Saith's eyes, as beautiful as they were, were distant. It was the same look my father had when he'd been diagnosed with cancer a few years ago. He beat it, but I still remember the sorrow in his eyes. It showed even during the times where he wanted to be strong for us.

"Go ahead. Ask."

"Ask what?"

"Why I'm in this chair. I won't be mad."

"Well, then, why don't you just tell me?"

I brushed my hair behind my ears and folded my legs under me.

"You gotta get all comfortable like that?"

I laughed. "You are something else, you know that?"

"I mean, you just gotta make a brother feel even more uncomfortable by crossing your legs in that crazy flexible way."

I looked down. I stopped smiling. "Oh, I mean, I wasn't trying to be inconsiderate, I just..."

I stopped when I realized he was smirking again. That smirk.

"Ha, ha. Real funny."

I laughed. Saith smiled, showing a hint of his dimple, then stopped. He went back to that same focused look he had before.

"So, what classes do you have?" I asked, changing the subject.

"I have four majors, Physics, Spanish 2, Pre-Calc and History. Art as a minor and another class."

"Which one?"

"Can't remember."

He stopped talking. "You?"

"The classes you took last year at whatever school you came from. Tenth-grade stuff."

He pushed his chair back and looked at me. "Are you always so cynical?"

"Yep. Just like my daddy."

His face softened. "You guys are lucky. Everybody knows the Clovers. "

I swallowed. I had no desire to discuss business, but it was something I'd gotten used to. How could you hide in a family that was worth billions and received national press? You couldn't.

"Yeah. Doesn't your dad have a business? I heard my mom talking about it before I came down."

"Urban Central."

"The magazine?"

"Yep. The magazine."

"Now, that's dope. I love creative stuff like that."

He smiled but looked down at his lap. I heard a noise coming from behind me. I turned around. A girl was standing there. Her eyes and nose told me they had to be related in some way.

"Hi. I'm Myla. Saith's cousin," she said, reaching her hand out. I shook it.

"Oh, so you don't have a choice but to be around him," I said, looking back at him before introducing myself. "Brelyn."

"Yep. I inherited him,"Myla teased.

Saith grunted as we shared a laugh.

"How was your nap?" he asked her.

"Good. I thought you guys had gone to get pizza without me."

Saith shook his head. "Nope. Just came to say hi to our new neighbors."

Myla smiled, but I noticed she kept staring at Saith. He gave her a stern look back. Whatever that look meant, Myla suddenly shut down.

"Well, I gotta go. See you later. It was nice meeting you, Brelyn."

And just as fast as she came, she was gone. I looked back at Saith, clearly confused about what had just happened.

"Myla is my cousin from my mother's side."

He said it so quietly, I almost had to ask him to repeat it. That's when I noticed.

"Where is your mother?"

He pushed back against the fountain and spun his chair around a few times. It was like he didn't hear me. He took an imaginary basketball and started taking fake shots.

"Dead."

He said it like it was nothing. As if that was normal – for a teenage boy's mother to be dead.

"Myla has a way of bringing it up at the oddest times. That's why I gave her that look before she had the chance to blurt it out."

"Were you gonna eventually say something? Not that it's any of my business, but it would've come up don't you think?"

He shrugged. "It is what it is."

He continued taking fake shots. Right before I was about to say something else, Emé's car pulled into our long driveway. I could feel my smile widen as I stood up. Desmond got out the car, and I ran to greet him. He wrapped his arm around my shoulder as we walked back to Saith.

"Hey. Saith, right?" Desmond asked, extending his hand to him. "My father called me and told me we had some more testosterone around. As you can see, we're outnumbered."

Saith laughed at my brother's joke, while Emé and I stuck our tongues out at them.

"Whatever," she said. "Nice to meet you, Saith. Welcome to the world of the rich or famous."

"Rich or famous?"

Desmond chuckled. "She's being sarcastic. This neighborhood is full of rich or famous people. Not everybody is both."

"Ditto," Saith said. I smiled. He seemed to be warming up to my siblings much quicker than he had warmed up to me.

"Brelyn, come inside and talk to your big sister," Emé said. I wrapped my arm around her waist and waved goodbye to Saith.

"See you, Monday."

He gave me a slight nod, but nothing more. I chuckled, thinking about the effect the men in my family had on guys. If he was scared that Desmond might give him the third degree, it served him right for thinking he could rattle me. I hadn't acknowledged it in front of him, but he was giving me this icy tone as if I had knocked on his front door and asked him to come out and play. I joked with him and tried to break that ice. I understood being new, and I never wanted people to feel like they had to bow down to us because of our name, but something about Saith's attitude told me I'd have to show him that I wasn't just a family name.

Chapter 3

Monday came quicker than I'd wanted it to, which meant seeing Saith again. Over the weekend, Cashmere asked me a bunch of questions about him since she was out on a date when they came over. I gave her the facts. Yes, he is cute. Yes, he is in a wheelchair, and yes, he is smart. The rest, she'd have to find out on her own. Cashmere was an over analyzer. The one where asking one hundred questions for every situation made perfect sense to her, but made us all feel like we weren't as concerned as we should be about a particular matter. When I was first diagnosed, she asked the doctor's questions that my parents hadn't even thought of.

Desmond's door was closed when I walked past it to go down and get breakfast. He was the only one with a car. Cashmere tried to ask a hundred questions about the purchase when my dad first bought it, but Papa Clover shut her down immediately. Our parents had a system. If we wanted to keep them off our backs, we followed along. We were children who still volunteered at hospitals and shelters; who still shopped at Old Navy and ate at chain restaurants. We put up more money than we spent and had to make sure we tithed ten percent to our church.

That meant, we each weren't going to be rolling around in our own car before our senior year. Desmond, being the oldest, had just gotten his car at the beginning of the school year. Cashmere insisted she was responsible and old enough, but my father stuck to his rule. She all but proved his point when Desmond let her drive the car one day, and she left her driver's license home. I laughed at the thought as I entered the kitchen where my mom stood at the counter, finishing up breakfast. I walked over and kissed her on the cheek.

"Pancakes and turkey bacon today," she said. "That's all I have time for before my meeting."

"With Bloomingdale's?"

"Yes."

I grabbed a plate and started helping out. "You excited?"

"If they accept these new pieces into their jewelry department, it will be perfect for the line. It'll set the tone for the rest of this year."

I nodded. She looked at my neck. When she stopped smiling, I realized I'd forgotten to put it on. I put the plate down and ran back upstairs, taking the back way. Even with fewer steps, I was winded. I grabbed the four leaf clover chain from my jewelry box and put it on, smiling at myself in the mirror. When I got back down, Cashmere was in the kitchen. I could see the gold glints from her chain from where I stood. She smiled at me, and I hugged her.

"You feeling okay?"

I nodded. "Better than ever."

I walked back over and finished making everyone's plate.

"Is Emé coming?" I asked my mom.

"No. Not this morning. She's busy with auditions."

19

I could tell by the way she rushed through her answer that that wasn't the real reason Emé wasn't coming. Cashmere raised an eyebrow at me, but I shrugged. She knew Emé and I were close, but she hadn't told me anything about not coming to breakfast. She lived twenty minutes from us and usually stopped by for breakfast on Mondays; however, she had missed the last few times. She'd come to pick us up and hang out, but she hadn't sat down with us to eat. Mama Clover turned to us and smiled.

"Sit. Eat. Now."

We did. Desmond came down a few minutes late. Mama gave Desmond a look. Cashmere and I chuckled as Mama sat down and joined us. I looked at the empty seat next to her.

"Papa?"

"He went out early."

Desmond kicked my foot lightly under the table. I continued to eat. At least my siblings felt what I was feeling. My father never missed breakfast with us either. He was the business – so whatever needed to be done would have to wait until he arrived or he would make sure someone else could run a meeting for him. That's why we always had breakfast at the same time – so he could get back to running the winery, and Mama could get back to designing her jewelry pieces.

"So are we just gonna ignore the fact that our big sister and our father aren't here for breakfast?" I asked. Desmond kicked me harder this time. I kicked him back.

"Stop, you two," Mama fussed. "What's the rule?"

Cashmere sighed. "We talk when everyone is here. No rumors. No gossip."

With that, we continued eating, making small talk about life and everything else except the two empty chairs that screamed at us the entire time we ate.

❉ ❉ ❉

I saw Saith as soon as Desmond pulled up. It was hard not to see him since he was the only person at our school in a wheelchair. The three of us walked over to him and Myla.

"Hey, Myla," I said. I didn't greet him until he was looking at me.

"Hey," he said first.

Surprised, I smiled. "What's up?"

Cashmere made her introduction, and we all headed in the same direction. Desmond took a look at Myla's schedule, which she had been trying to read for the last few minutes.

"You're in ninth," he said. "So you're on the third floor."

"I have to walk all the way to the third floor alone?" she asked.

"You're a big girl, right? You wanted to wear makeup this morning," Saith teased. She gave him a death stare. He bowed his head and sighed. I could see that he was still smiling, though.

"I'll walk you," I chimed in.

Saith and Desmond went down the hall, and I grabbed Myla's arm to walk to my locker.

"My locker is on this floor. My first class is on the second," I said as Cashmere grabbed my hand.

Myla stared at us for a second.

"What?"

"You guys always hold hands on your way to class?"

I looked down. I felt sarcasm ready to escape my lips, but Cashmere broke the silence before I could unleash it.

"Yeah. If Desmond were still walking with us, he'd be in the center."

I looked at her and winked. Not many understood our bond. We grew up in an area where the idea of family unity

21

seemed to be foreign; therefore, many treated us like foreigners. It could've been my father's upbringing down on Diamond Street in North Philadelphia or my mother's upbringing in the rough streets of Brooklyn that led them to instill in each of us the appreciation for family unity. More often than not, most people expected us to be closed off, bourgeoisie or too caught up in our billion-dollar world to consider spending time together or to truly get to know one another. But this was us – no cover ups, no airbrushed ambiance – we just were. At that moment, I realized how silly it was for me to be annoyed with Myla for judging our close-knit bond. With everything going on in my life, I just hit a nerve. I couldn't seem to bring myself to trust that with or without a business, my family would love me the same. I mean, I knew they *would*, I just wouldn't fit in.

As soon I arrived outside of my first-period class, I caught a glimpse of Marcus who flirts with me from time to time. A part of me liked him and his innocent flirting, but I kept it to myself. My diagnosis had completely given me permission to be a punk in circumstances like this, and I was okay with it.

"Hey, Bre," he greeted, walking closer to me before we entered our class.

"Hey. You good?"

"Yeah," he said. "I was thinking of hitting Mickey's Pizza after school. You down?"

"Uh, let me see what Cashmere is doing, and I'll let you know."

He stood there as if he was waiting for me to change my mind. When I didn't say anything else, he walked inside. I followed behind him. As soon as I sat down, I felt myself falling asleep. It was crazy how the nine hours of sleep my doctor recommended seemed to only make me more tired than

I was before the disease. Somehow, I made it through the class without my head hitting the desk. Science was easy for me. I often found myself getting excited about formulas and figuring out how the human body worked. It was the other stuff that I found to be boring. English was cool when we focused on the occasional classic that I loved, like last week's reading of *The Joys of Motherhood*. Because we went to a business academy, we were forced to take two courses that were tailored around math and business – one of which was the required math and the other, a class of your choice. This year I'd decided on Entrepreneurship. Of course, that was in September. I got diagnosed in November. Here it was five months later, and the business I'd come up with was looking like a flop.

Walking to my locker, I got excited at the thought of meeting Marcus after school. But whether he liked it or not, Cashmere would have to come. I could date alone next year when I was sixteen. For the most part, dating wasn't even an issue with my parents – our name just made us vulnerable, causing their protective nature to be at level one hundred. I felt my bag vibrating. As I reached around to pull out my cell phone, it hit me before I even opened it. I looked at the text on the screen. *Doctor's appointment at three. Don't forget. Mama.* How could I? She'd beat it into my head and my calendar ever since the appointment had been made. Even though it was just a regular check-up, I was surprised she was letting me go alone.

The day flowed by pretty quick. As soon as two thirty approached, I prepared to head out the door. The bell rang just as I closed my locker. Cashmere was at her after school business class while Desmond was probably shooting hoops at school until I was done.

"You know Mom told us to go with you," Cashmere said as soon as she saw me.

"Yep. But just like you guys sneak and do your own thing sometimes, I need to do mine."

"Dating and making out isn't the same as a health issue," she shot back.

"I'm going by myself," I said, not even looking at her.

She was silent.

"Marcus wanted to go for pizza."

She beamed. "What did you say?"

"Nothing. I told him I'd let him know. But, that was before I remembered the appointment."

"You can still go. I'll cover for you," she said, a little too excited. Cashmere was in the dating stage of life, so her excitement usually trickled over into trying to get me to date sooner than I wanted to. I could only imagine the scene they would cause if my parents knew that she'd been on a few dates before her sixteenth birthday. My choice was to wait. Marcus was cute – but he wasn't worth Desmond's nor Papa Clover's wrath; especially since I'd been under extra protection since November. Besides, sneaking may have come easy for Cashmere, but it would be a chore for me.

"I gotta go. See you in a few," I shouted over my shoulder as I walked off. The hospital was only a block from our school, which made this section of Lafayette Hill one of the busiest intersections ever. Once inside, I still had ten minutes to spare, so I grabbed my science book and started on some of my homework. Just as my name was called, I stood up too quickly and dropped my book. When I bent to pick it up, I felt the sharpest pain shoot up my back. I closed my eyes, refusing to scream out. I held the scream in until I could feel the surge of electricity that had gone through my body subside. When I stood back up, the receptionist was looking at me like I had three heads.

"I'm okay. Just got lost in this science," I said, giving her a stern look. Don't cry, Bre. Don't cry.

Unfortunately for me, the doctor's exam was so thorough, I could barely hide the pain while he poked and prodded me. It just laid in waiting until he tapped on my spine. I winced.

"How's the medication?" Dr. Ross asked.

"Great."

"Brelyn..."

I sighed. "It's good. I do have some pain from time to time, but otherwise, everything is fine."

"When was the last time you had any pain?"

I gave him a funny look. He forced a smiled.

"That recent, huh?"

"In the waiting room."

After I had explained what happened, he made me lie down and go through a deeper examination. It wasn't invasive, but I knew he'd call my parents. On the flip side – I would've told them anyway. It was in our blood to be strong. Tough. But I was still the baby, and there were times I knew my mother's arms were everything I needed.

❧ ❧ ❧

As I was leaving the hospital, I called Mama.

"Hey, baby," she said. The minute I heard her voice, I cracked.

"Mama, I was in pain today. Just a little, but it hurt."

Silence. Then I heard her swallow. "Baby, where are Cashmere and Desmond?"

"I wouldn't let them come. Don't be upset."

More silence. Then, I heard her talking to Papa Clover in the background.

"We're coming to meet you. Stay there."

"No. Mom, no. Don't. Please."

"Watch your tone," she said. "I didn't *ask* you. I said we're coming to get you."

And that was it. The call was over. I didn't want Cashmere and Desmond to get in trouble. I texted Desmond late last night that if he didn't let me go alone, I was going to call Kelly and tell her he'd gone on a date with Marissa. I loved my brother, but I was desperate.

I walked back to the school at a slower pace. The pain was gone, but the feeling I had in the pit of my stomach was growing by the second. I called Cashmere.

"Mom and Dad are coming."

"What happened?" she yelled.

"Don't yell at me, but I called to tell Mom about the visit."

"And you couldn't wait until we got home?"

I hung up. There was nothing more to say. I waited outside for my parents to come. Cashmere kept calling me, but I didn't answer. Just as my father's Denali turned the corner, I saw Saith rolling towards me. I looked away, ready now more than ever to get this day over with.

"Hey, baby Clover," he said.

I turned to face him. "That's not my name, it's Brelyn. I'll even take Bre, but *don't* ever call me baby Clover." I stepped closer to his legs. I was standing over him with fire in my eyes. "Got it?"

For the first time since Saith and I had encountered each other, he hesitated before saying something back.

"My bad," he said. "Don't bite my head off."

My father's truck came to a slow crawl. I could feel the tears coming before I even felt Papa's hand grab mine.

"Let's go, baby girl."

My mother came around the other side and grabbed my backpack. My father scooped me in his arms as my mother

26

rubbed my back. He laid me on the backseat. My mother slid in next to me. I sat up, irked that all of this happened in front of the new boy next door. The boy whose dimples had made me feel a certain kind of way. The boy who would now know that something was wrong. I saw him staring at us as the truck pulled away. Even through the tinted windows, I knew he was staring at me.

At that moment, I felt my mother's hand on my leg. I reached for my phone, turning it away from her view, and texted Marcus. *Can't make it. Sorry. Maybe some other time.* I turned to face her. Without another word, I scooted closer to her; close enough that I could feel her heart beating against my ear. The truth – I didn't want to die. No matter how tough I pushed myself to be and how much strength I wanted people to see, I couldn't control my body. The disease could possibly kill me and every time I felt an inch of pain, I felt just a little closer to death. Although I knew I had a milder form of lupus, it was still a disease that could affect any of my organs at any given moment. Knowing this disease affected my immune system the most is what scared me – the flu could cause major problems. Essentially, dialysis could be in my near future. That's if I had a future to look forward to.

Chapter 4

Dinner was better than I'd expected. Papa hadn't said a word to Desmond, at least not in front of the family. Mama asked Cashmere never to listen to me again, but other than that, everything was good. The baked chicken and famous creamed corn Mom made, along with the buttermilk biscuits and a tossed salad, seemed to have everyone in heaven. Even Emé was here tonight. I sat next to her, excited that my big sister had joined us.

"Okay, I have an announcement," Mama said. "Everyone quiet down."

My father placed his cell phone back in his pocket. Cashmere and Emé stopped mid-sentence, and my brother stopped eating.

"Bloomingdale's said 'yes,'" my mother said, with a straight face.

I screamed, jumping up to hug her. "You held out on me," I teased.

"Yes. I wanted the family to hear it all at once," she said, looking at my father. I looked over at him. I saw him wink at her and smile.

Their love for each other was sickening most of the time, unbelievable the rest. My siblings saw it too, which is why I didn't understand Cashmere's need to be so free with the guys she dated, but, to each his or her own.

"So, when do we get to see the designs for the summer line?" Emé asked giving Mama a serious look.

"Soon, but I want to have full confirmation on the chosen designs before I show you," Mom said.

My mother's hand was still wrapped around mine. I felt the way she clinched it. It was as if she wanted to say something different than what she said. I was uneasy at the thought. I had never known her to be anything other than direct. Whatever was going on between her and Emé had her acting slightly different than normal, but I knew better than to ask. It would come out eventually. Emé and I were closer than Cashmere and I. I guess it was because she was the oldest and brought balance to the teenage tendencies that we all had in the house. When I was first diagnosed, Emé's reaction had been worse than my mother's – at least in the emotional aspect. Part of me knew that things with my mother and sister would always be a little tense since Emé didn't belong to her biologically. She loved her like she was her own, but every so often, Emé found a way to remind her that she wasn't hers.

"So, this means what for us?" Cashmere asked. "Are we selling your pieces to some of our friends' parents? Do we need to create order forms? How can we push the envelope, Mom?"

As always, Cashmere was overthinking. Desmond looked at me and stuck his finger down his throat, faking sickness. My father crossed his eyes. I laughed.

"Cash, we'll figure all that out later," Mama replied.

When dinner was over, I ran upstairs to take a bath. Mama had prepared the nicest oatmeal and peppermint bathwater. It smelled great, but it was also a great way to relax my muscles. The Jacuzzi in my bathroom gave me the right amount of privacy that allowed me to focus on another journal entry once I was finished with my bath. I re-read my last entry before I jumped into the tub.

March 28, 2016

I'm not sure if it's my fear of dying or just my fear of not leaving something amazing behind. Whatever it is, I'm not too anxious to know either way. Because leaving something behind would require me to die, also. Cashmere has her t-shirts. Desmond has his sneakers. Emé has acting and her skin care line. Papa has his wine. Mama has her jewelry. Brelyn has lupus. Sure, I'm not all lupus, but God, during this time in my life, when I was just about to embark on a journey of business – one where I know I'd soar, this comes over me. Even as a Christian I don't get how I'm supposed to learn anything from this. I want to trust this whole faith thing, and I will because I know nothing else. But what's the reality that I'll live to be able to tell a greater story? Lying down to sleep has its pain moments. Getting up just to get dressed brings about a duty fit for a burlesque dancer trying to fit into twenty bodysuits to look right for the stage.

I gently closed my journal as I pondered where I'd stopped my entry only a few days ago. It was the first week of April, and we were just a few months from finishing the school year. I stripped naked and slid down into the tub, carefully making sure my hair was securely tucked under my bonnet. My sister had curled it for me this morning. She'd walked in when I was struggling with the flat irons even though I'd curled it to perfection just the day before. I let the peppermint seep into my body as I laid back. Whatever pain I'd been feeling at the doctor's office slowly subsided as I bathed. I left it all there in the tub.

❦❦❦

An hour after taking my bath, I stepped outside to get some fresh air before heading to bed. I looked over and noticed Saith was outside. I was reluctant to go over, especially since I'd all but spit in his face earlier.

"How was your first day?" I asked, now standing a few feet away from him.

"We're friends again?"

He kept throwing small rocks at the fountain in his courtyard, but never once turned to face me.

"I didn't know we were friends to begin with," I shot back.

There was a sense of defiance on my end – but that's what made the moment so special. If he wanted to push, I would push back.

"You're a piece of work, you know that?"

"Me? You don't say," I mocked him.

He glared at me for a second. He placed his left hand on the wheel and proceeded to go back so that he was closer to his home.

"Girls are such a trip."

I slowly followed behind. "I've been around the world."

He stopped. I stopped. I could see a small vein in his neck throbbing. He slowly turned back toward me. He cut his eyes at me. I was standing there with the largest smile on my face that I could muster up. It was close to nine, and I would have to go in soon. I just wanted to get this over with, because I knew he would ask. His rock hard expression began to transform into a blush, then a laugh. A hearty laugh. It was music to my ears.

"I don't know what to do with you," he joked. "If you didn't have a big brother, I'd..."

I raised an eyebrow. "You'd have to deal with the Papa bear."

"True. But I've dodged plenty of those. No big deal." He wiped fake sweat from his brow.

"You still never said what you'd do?"

"I'd throw you over my shoulder and spin you around until you got dizzy."

Not what I was expecting. I was just about to ask Saith why didn't he do it when he started rolling towards me. He stopped at my feet.

"You'd have to try to lift me to do something like that."

"Five bucks says I can; ten says I can spin you. A full thirty seconds and I get twenty."

"Let's make it an even hundred-dollar bet. Thirty seconds."

He gave me a sneaky look – and then he did the unexpected. He adjusted his chair a little, then came toward me and grabbed my legs. I had no time to scream. I let out a little yelp, but before I knew it, he had already started counting. No roller coaster ride could've prepared me for this. I was hanging over his shoulder as he counted and I joined in. Thirty seconds never felt so good. When he placed me gently back on my feet, I stumbled. A lot. I was just about to hit the ground when he grabbed me by my waist and sat me on the armrest of his chair.

I looked at him, breathing heavy and I caught myself from wanting to wipe the little sweat that had broken out on his face away. I was breathless but not as winded as I thought I'd be.

"How in the world do you do that? I thought you were paralyzed."

"Partially and it's temporary. I can still function. I just can't walk."

I stood up, finally able to stand up straight without feeling like the earth was giving away beneath me.

"How did it happen? You in the chair I mean?"

I hadn't meant for it to come out so bluntly, but what else could I do. It was blaring at me.

"Car accident. No big deal."

"Wow. Sorry to hear that. Did you play a lot before it happened?"

"Play?"

"Basketball. The shirt you had on."

He relaxed. "Oh, yeah. Every day. Basketball was my everything." He paused again.

"Mine too. In a way."

He looked at me. "Why were you leaving the hospital today? Did you get sick at school or something?"

I didn't say anything. I just walked over and sat down at the edge of our shrubbery. The air was cooler by the fountain. I was quiet, something that wasn't normal for me. But the words just wouldn't come out.

"Okay," he said, startling me. "If you don't want to tell me, I understand. But that tells me it's bigger than just the effects of a bad school lunch."

I forced a smile. "Nobody eats the school lunch. And you shouldn't either."

"Awww, she cares about me," he said, throwing his hand over his heart.

"Did you sign up for drama, too?"

He scrunched his face up at me and stuck out his tongue.

"I have lupus."

I knew he'd heard me, because he rolled his chair back a little, then came closer than he had been before.

"The disease?"

I looked at him with more fire than I had the first time he'd gotten smart with me.

"Whoa, before you snap on me and start World War III, I was only asking because my aunt has it. You definitely deal with it well."

My face softened. "What makes you think I'd start the third World War?"

He gave me a quizzical look. "So you don't remember almost knocking me out of my chair this afternoon when you were getting into your parent's truck?"

I giggled. "Oh. Well, about that..."

"Don't apologize."

"I wasn't. I was just going to say that was a much smaller battle."

And then we both laughed. We laughed until tears came out of our eyes and I was able to see the possibility of a great friendship in the making. A friendship that might be worth exploring.

As our laughter softened, I could see understanding in Saith's eyes as he returned to the topic of my lupus. "I won't say that I'm sorry to hear about your illness because I know you've heard it a thousand times," he said. "But, I know you're strong enough to fight it."

I played with my clover chain.

"How do you know that?"

He put his hand on my knee, causing me to look into his eyes. "Because I see it. The same way I know you didn't feel pity for me when you saw my chair."

I cocked my head to the side. I felt my lips curling upward. I tried to suppress it. "Whatever. Don't be tryna figure me out."

I turned away so he wouldn't see the smile, but it was too late.

"I think I already have, Ms. Brelyn. Wait...it is okay to call you that, right?"

I stood up. "Maybe. I'll let you know tomorrow."

My phone was vibrating. I knew it was my alarm letting me know it was time to go to bed. I had scheduled sleep times so I wouldn't be so drowsy the next day.

"Is that a promise?" Saith asked me as I turned to walk in the house.

I looked back at him. He winked. *Damn, those eyes.*

"Yes. It is."

❀ ❀ ❀

Before I knew it, it was Saturday again. I got excited thinking about my day with Emé. She'd been so busy in the last month our private time together had been somewhat limited, but I texted her and made her promise that today wouldn't change. It wasn't a special day, but Saturdays were when she had the time, and I didn't have school.

We pulled up at Spruce Street Harbor Park. Since the park opened back up in the spring, people were flooding the place. When we entered, we headed straight for the hammocks. It was a ritual at this point – to lie in a hammock together and talk about life. Then, we'd go to one of the food trucks and eat, play ping pong or row in one of the boats. Most of the hammocks had been taken although it was only noon, but my eyes caught one off to the side that looked like it was waiting just for us. It was one of the larger ones. I ran over to it before anyone could grab it with Emé was right on my heels.

"Okay. I'll get in first, and then you lean into me," she said. It was a joke she always told me to make me comfortable. I'd fallen the first time we both tried to get in one together.

"Ha, ha. Bet you I can handle it better than you."

I got in first, gently and held the sides open so she could join me. She laughed when she saw how sturdy I kept the hammock.

"Okay. I see you've got your groove. Nice."

She threw her long brown hair up in a quick bun and laid back. I put my head on her shoulder.

"So, what's up with you and Mom?"

She sighed. "Damn it, Brelyn."

"You knew I was going to ask."

"Can we start with something lighter? How's school?" She sat up a little. "And why don't you tell me about this new neighbor."

I stared up at the clouds.

"What about him?"

"I hear he has a female cousin living with him. Why aren't you befriending her?"

"Who said I wasn't?"

"Because, every time you are outside, you're talking to him."

I sat up slowly. "So you and Mom can find the time to discuss me, but you can't discuss what's going on between the two of you?"

"She didn't tell me."

"Lies. I know she did."

Emé laid back down. I followed suit.

"My auditions are driving me crazy, and with the upcoming opening of the DermaSpa with Noni, I feel overwhelmed. That's all."

"Well, since you asked," I said, ready to change the subject. I knew when someone was feeding me bologna. "Saith is a cool guy. Nothing major. But he was in a car accident. That's how he ended up in the chair."

"You like him?"

I sighed, taking a moment before I answered. "I said he was a cool guy."

"But you stalled for so long, there must be something."

I didn't want to tell her anything. For one, it was clear my mother had been telling her that Saith and I were spending nights outside speaking to each. Two, Cashmere's tendencies to get caught up with a guy had everyone on edge about me – feeling like they needed to be *extra* careful so that the baby didn't become a statistic. My mind was saying 'no,' but my heart, the part of me that Emé had, was saying it was okay to be transparent with my big sister at this moment.

"Honestly, we've only talked three or four times. I'll let you know if I start catching feelings."

She smiled. "Saith is a cutie. I saw those dimples."

I blushed. I couldn't help it. Emé looked at me and pinched my nose. I laughed.

"Did you see those eyes, too?" I asked.

Chapter 5

My day with Emé ended sooner than I'd wanted, but she'd gotten a call from her agent about one of her auditions. As soon as I got home, I decided to start working on ideas for a new business that wouldn't require so much of me physically. My mother suggested an online platform for children dealing with lupus – which I wasn't sure how I would monetize that. My brother asked if I wanted to make a female sneaker for Bricks, which honestly didn't sound so bad, especially with my love for fitness. A fitness sneaker down the line made sense. Cashmere wanted me in on the t-shirt brand when she first started, and she still had my name on one of her business plans.

Nonetheless, I felt that market was saturated, and too many people our age had a T-shirt or clothing line of some kind. Cashmere was great at her business, but I also knew that my parents' name had a lot to do with it growing faster than the average start-up. If I could just find something that fit me, something that no one could take away or diminish the Clover flair that I'd put into it. That type of business would set my soul on fire, so as long as it involved my love for fitness.

I looked around my room at the Nike posters, the posters of my favorite athletes and all the fitness gear I'd accrued over the years – the barbells engraved with my name in the corner of my room, resting nicely against a purple basketball that sat in a glass case; the T-shirts with fitness slogans that I'd hung on my wall and the banner that read "Bodies by Brelyn". I missed it all, and I couldn't just give it up. I needed to find a way to incorporate fitness back into my daily life. I sat down at my computer and opened a blank document. I started typing.

Bodies by Brelyn

Twenty minutes later, *Bodies By Brelyn* still sat alone on the screen. Just as I was about to start typing again, I received a notification letting me know that I had a new email. I wanted to ignore it since I was trying my best to get in a zone, but I was curious. When I opened it, I felt a smile creeping onto my face. I'd given Saith my email address when we were in school, just to see if it would spark something. It did.

Bre,

You gave me your email address. So, I'm emailing you. What are you doing tonight? How are classes going?

Saith

I burst out laughing. He was clearly much better at talking in person than he was with writing emails. I wanted to be petty and write back how wonderful the two lines he'd managed to muster up were, but I decided to make both of us laugh instead.

Saith,

I'm writing something right now. Classes suck. You?

Bre

PS Some conversations are so much better in person. Why don't you come knock on the door, and we can talk in the courtyard?

The last line didn't register until I'd already hit send. I realized I had just invited Saith to my front door, and I was upstairs ready for bed. I didn't know if he would show up or not, but I wanted to be the one to open the door if he did. I threw on a pair of yoga pants, sneakers and a jacket. Just for my mother's sake, I threw on a cap. Until it was blazing hot outside, she would be concerned about me getting chills. I also knew when summer came, she'd be concerned about me passing out from heat and exhaustion. Chuckling, I grabbed my cell phone and headed downstairs.

My parents were in the ballroom dancing. No one else was home. I grabbed the handle of our large oak door and swung it open just as Saith was about to knock. He grinned when he saw me standing there.

"You just get done working out?"

He noticed. "No. I just love fitness."

"I can tell."

I closed the door, and we went over to the fountain. I sat down.

"How?"

"Okay, let's see," he said, rolling back so he could see me clearly. He locked his wheels in place and began counting down on his fingers. "You have a Nike Fitness case on your cell phone. Your book bag is a retro Nike book bag. Your sister mentioned something about you working out again when we were in school on Thursday and, for the sake of not coming off like I'm flirting, I did notice that you're in pretty good shape." He paused. "Considering what you shared I mean."

I was speechless. It was crazy to me how he'd been able to pick up on all that. Especially since Cashmere's comment came and went so quickly that I hadn't even heard her until Saith had asked her to repeat herself. My book bag was a gift from one of my dad's friends who worked at Nike and the case, well, I always had my cell phone with me. It would be hard to miss, but still.

"You get no cool points for thinking you know me," I said smiling. He winked, and I relaxed. We talked until close to ten o'clock. For some reason, getting nine hours of sleep tonight wasn't so important to me at that moment.

❦ ❦ ❦

Sunday was what I considered to be my refresh day. I got to recharge for the week, rest, read my Bible and scribble away in my prayer journal. It was also the day I didn't do anything that would take away my focus on having a positive week. Growing up in Philadelphia had its challenges – the constant cycle of bad news, the fear that one of my siblings wouldn't make it home safe, and going to school and hearing about another student who had gotten murdered. Granted we lived in a nice neighborhood, and we didn't live right inside of Philadelphia, our roots were there. We had family all throughout, and we did most of our summer cookouts right where my father had grown up.

We saw the looks every time we went back. The looks that told us we no longer belonged and that look that read 'they came to slum so they would feel better about their tax write offs.' Sadly, we got the same looks when we went to visit Mama's family in Brooklyn. Her parents loved their Brooklyn brownstone and refused to move. Since her father was now a minister, he definitely wasn't interested in moving and leaving his church behind.

We were members of a church but didn't go every Sunday. I enjoyed bedside Baptist moments even more than going to service. I could figure out what God was saying without all the hoopla and hollering that took place behind me in the pews. Reading the Bible from the comfort of my room, suited me just fine. Just as I was about to finish reading one of my favorite Psalms, I heard a knock at my door.

"Come in," I murmured.

It would either be Mama or Papa. My siblings were doing their own thing in their rooms.

"Hey, baby girl," my father said, opening the door slightly. "You got a minute for your old man?"

I smiled. "Now, you know I would never tell you no."

He winked. "Come to the office."

I closed my books and slid off my bed. He opened the door all the way and took my hand in his. We entered his office, which was probably bigger than the Oval Office and sat down. I picked up the golden Earth that sat on his desk and started passing it back and forth between my hands. He cleared his throat. I put it back.

"What's up, Papa?

"You want to talk about what's going on with you," he said, leaning forward. His salt and pepper goatee looked sharper than it had two days ago, which means the barber had been here. "And don't give me no BS, Bre."

I sat back in the chair. I was calm. No need to panic.

"Are you talking about the lupus or Saith?"

He squinted his eyes at me. "Let's talk about both."

I shook my head and sighed. "Papa, I've never lied to you before, and I won't start now."

He leaned back again, more relaxed than before. I could tell he was still a little uptight by the way he kept folding and unfolding his hands.

"Good, because your sister has me ready to pull all my gray hairs out," he said, forcing a joke.

"Well, what do you want to talk about first?"

He raised an eyebrow at me.

"Dad, he's just the new neighbor –"

"Who you've been getting extremely friendly with. You let him spin you around on his chair? Bre..."

I tried not to show my irritation, but I could feel my nostrils flaring before he could even finish his statement.

"Mama..."

"No. Me. I saw you, Bre. Do you think I work so much that I don't know what's going on with my baby girl?"

I felt tears welling up in my eyes. "I know you know. I just don't get why I'm treated like such a baby."

"Because you are the baby."

"The baby who noticed your treatment of me changed when I got sick," I said, crossing my arms. "Cashmere is the one you should be concerned about."

His nostrils flared this time. "I am. Trust me, but I'm concerned about *all* my children, including your brother."

I dropped my arms. "What's going on with Desmond?"

"Mind yours," he scolded. "Tell me this. Do you really think that I'm treating you differently because you're sick? Even if you weren't, I would still watch you from the window. Especially now that some boy's involved."

His voice was getting deeper.

"It was bad enough with me just being the baby. Now, I'm the *sickly* baby, and you guys can't even let me go to my doctor's visits alone."

Big mistake. That last visit didn't actually go so well, but instead of my father getting upset, he closed his eyes.

"You have no idea what my life would be like if you weren't in it," he confessed. He said it like it was normal, but my father very rarely shared his feelings other than the everyday 'I love you.' Even when he did have cancer, he toughed it out, prayed a lot and just went harder with his healthy eating and working out. Mama said he cried once, and that was because she mentioned us when he was at chemo. To this day, he doesn't know that I know he cried.

"So you're scared too, huh?"

He opened his eyes. "Brelyn, I'm human. Not a robot, and you're my daughter."

"Papa, you never have to prove your love to me," I said, wiping at a tear. "I know you love me. That's no question. I just wish you would trust me."

He stared at me for a minute, then leaned forward and grabbed my hands.

"Baby, I trust you," he said. He stood up and walked over to the window. He pointed outside to the world. "It's them that I don't trust."

❧ ❧ ❧

I plopped down on Desmond's bed as he sat at his desk sketching new designs. There were times I'd just come in and sit with him, just to see him do his thing. We didn't have to actively do anything together for me to enjoy spending time with him.

"What's up with you and Dad?"

He stopped sketching. "What makes you think something is up?"

I watched as his dimples deepened and then disappeared. He chewed gum harder than I worked out. I was sure of it.

"Desmond, come on. It's Dad. No family secrets, remember."

"He wants me to start preparing for the family business."

"Isn't that what you want?" I placed my legs under me and got comfortable. Desmond smiled at me.

"Young lad, you don't know everything," he joked. "I want to be an entrepreneur. Nobody said I wanted to take over the winery."

"But you wouldn't have to do it right away. He just means when he..."

He looked at me. "I know that's what he means. I just want him to give me a chance to want it. Right now, he's shoving it down my throat."

I had to agree with Desmond there. My father was adamant that Desmond, Jr. would be the one to hold the reigns after he left this Earth. He had started preparing him a year ago. Cancer had shaken him up some. I think Desmond did it out of obligation, but once my dad was well and moving around like normal, Desmond had started pulling away.

"Have you told him you may not want to run it?"

Desmond cut his eyes at me. "Are you really my baby sister?"

I threw a dirty sock at him. "I'm just asking. I know how we all want to please our parents."

"No," he said, getting up and sitting next to me on the bed. "*You* want to please our parents. The rest of us are doing just fine doing our own thing."

I pushed him. "What the hell is that supposed to mean?"

"It means we've all been there," he said. "Even Emé, but it doesn't mean you'll stay there."

He wrapped his arm around me and pulled me against him. "Be brave, Bre. Don't think about your disease stopping you. Don't think about our parents stopping you. Just be brave."

Desmond kissed my cheek and stood up. He walked over to his walk in closet. When he came back out, he had a ball in his hand.

"I am brave," I said, standing up. I already knew why he'd gotten the ball.

"You know I believe in you right?"

I nodded. "Ditto, kiddo."

He walked back over to me. "First to twenty wins."

"You really want to do my laundry next weekend?"

"You claiming you'll win?"

I winked at him and grabbed the ball. "When have I ever lost?"

Chapter 6

Later in the week, I sat in math class staring at the paper in front me. I hated failing, even in times when I knew without a doubt that I hadn't properly prepared. That was exactly the case with my last math test which as it turned out was was harder than I anticipated. The red B minus marked at the top of the paper had taunted me since my teacher returned the test. Some would say a B-minus was great, but to me, it was yet another reminder of the recent changes in my life. My 3.7 GPA was gradually slipping from my grasp. Naturally, part of the issue stemmed from hospital stays, but much of it was just me giving in to the notion that I just might not be around long enough to attend college. I blame my attitude on my own curiosity – of course, my online research after my diagnosis returned all of the worst case scenarios. It was disheartening to see that there were cases where someone died as early as eighteen or twenty. I'd let it all psych me out, and now I was paying for it. When I looked back down at the B-minus again, I knew I would have to get it together.

In my family, it was a given that the Clover children earned nothing less than a B, and that was pushing it. Last year, when Cashmere brought home a C-plus during the first quarter of the year, my dad took her laptop. Education was important, and although he didn't pressure any of us to go to college, he urged us to walk in excellence. He commanded it with his own presence. Thankfully, I still had all A's and B's and even though this was just one test, my father's expectations rang in my head.

❊ ❊ ❊

Later in the day, after school, I faced another test courtesy of Cashmere. She sat on my bed pestering me in her attempts to find out what Saith and I talked about when we were alone. If only she knew how good our conversations really were. In fact, they were beyond good, they were great. Whether he knew it or not, he was able to put a smile on my face even when I wasn't in the mood. He called me every night to talk. Our conversations were full and covered everything from sports to health, his and mine. I even suggested a few conditioning exercises he could do while in his chair that would possibly speed up his recovery. I was no doctor, but if he had the faith to work towards walking again, I had the faith to back him up.

"Well, if you won't tell me what you guys talk about, at least tell me about the new business plan that's been sitting on your desk," she said, rotating the book so she could take a better look. I jumped up and grabbed it from her.

"You suck, you know that? Why are you so nosy?" I yelled, with laughter in my voice.

"Because I'm everything a big sister should be – cute and nosy."

"We'll debate on the cute part later," I teased, plopping down on her lap. "I actually wanted your opinion on this. I know you'll ask me all the right questions to make sure I have all of my bases covered."

She pinched me.

"Ouch." I mugged her in return.

"Okay, enough. I have a date in an hour, so what's up?"

It was my turn to give her a curious look, but I'd given up on trying to figure out Cashmere's dating life a long time ago.

"So, I was thinking of revamping Bodies by Brelyn to an online platform where people can take virtual classes and have the benefit of health and fitness resources for a monthly fee." I stood up and turned the page in my notebook, ready to take notes. "This way, I can keep doing what I love, put it on a website and still make some money. I know it'll take some time, but, it's a business." In my heart of hearts it wasn't exactly what I envisioned for Bodies by Brelyn, but at this point, I was willing to try anything. I shrugged nonchalantly to mask my anticipation of Cashmere's opinion. Luckily it didn't take long before she responded.

"I like it. But have you thought about how you're going to present it to your former customers who enjoyed your live classes?" she asked thoughtfully before continuing. "I would even consider an option where you could offer limited face-to-face training sessions with a select number of clients, but on a much more scaled down basis. You know, so if they wanted to, they could take advantage of both options. You could take on as few as four clients a month, and it wouldn't be too strenuous on you."

I wasted no time writing down all of Cashmere's suggestions; they were brilliant. I leaned towards her and pointed to the section of my plan that outlined the proposed format of the online classes. "What about the format? You think it's too much?"

"Not at all. It will definitely take some organization on your part, but it's definitely doable," Cashmere said encouragingly. "I think if you offered the virtual classes along with optional packages for people who want to meet with you privately you would be set. Especially if you also helped online clients put together fitness goals? I've seen some similar offers on Instagram lately."

My head snapped up at her last comment, and I stopped writing. "So then what would make me different?"

"Your story," she said, pushing her short freshly colored hair behind her ear. "You can't be afraid to tell your story, especially at your age." Cashmere paused as the gravity of mystery weighed upon her. "Plus, I don't know any normal fifteen-year-olds that love fitness the way you do."

I stuck my tongue out at her. "I am normal."

She laughed. "Girl, you talk more about eating right and working out than Jillian Michaels. There's *nothing* normal about that."

"There's nothing normal about dating guys who are four years older than you either, but I keep my lips sealed."

She stopped smiling.

As soon as the words crossed my lips, I knew that I had said too much. I hadn't meant to hit that far below the belt, but lately, I'd been running out of ammunition when it came to teasing my siblings. I could see a mixture of hurt and defiance flash across her eyes.

"He's only three years older, and that was one time," she said defensively.

"Cash, I was kidding. My bad, okay?" I hated that I had hurt her feelings, but the truth of the matter was I didn't like what she was doing. She was too good for all of it, but I knew regardless of what I said to her today, Cashmere would do what she wanted to do. At this point, it would take a sign from God to slow her down. I steered the conversation back to business.

"So, you think that I should let the *world* know that I'm sick?" I wasn't too sure how I felt about that, and I definitely didn't want to use pity as a marketing tool.

Her face softened. "Yes. Brelyn, it's not AIDS. I'm not saying that to be cruel, but you know what I mean." She pulled her vibrating cell phone from her back pocket. "Sometimes you act like you were given a death sentence."

Had I heard her correctly? "Excuse me? There isn't a cure for this you know." I waited for her response, willing it to show more compassion than her last statement.

"Yes. I know. I read the brochures and asked a gazillion questions, remember?" Cashmere said, standing up. "All I'm saying is own it. Use it. It's your power. Look at how the local paper covered Dad's story when he had cancer. It was monumental."

I did remember. They'd done a write up on his business and how amazing it was for a man of color, even though they didn't use those exact words, to be such a force in the wine and distillery business. He was breaking records that his white counterparts had taken quadruple generations to achieve. When they ran the story, he had just recovered from cancer, and for lack of a better term, cancer was familiar. People all over the globe and of all ages knew about cancer or had been affected by it in some way. Lupus was different. It was known, but not in the same manner as cancer. I stopped myself before continuing my thoughts. *Was I really making this a popularity contest between cancer and lupus?* I shook the thoughts out my head and returned to Cashmere.

"I don't know Cashmere, opening myself up to the public is an entirely different ballgame." Of course, many of my former clients know I have lupus, but I was in no way ready to put myself on blast all over social media. "Don't we already get enough attention?"

She shrugged. "You're right about that. Like these crazy comments on the picture I posted of us yesterday."

She turned her phone so I could see. I shook my head. "Haters."

She laughed. "Exactly. But if they aren't talking about you, you aren't doing something right." She started towards the door. "And they hated Jesus. Look at his legacy."

I smirked at my sister's last comment. I knew if the man upstairs knew what she was doing lately, she would think differently of her latest date. As she left my room, I watched her take a call and dismiss our conversation. I turned back to my desk and began incorporating all of the ideas from our conversation into my business plan. Cashmere had definitely helped me. Most importantly she made me realize that I had to come to terms with the reality of the role lupus would play in Bodies by Brelyn. Even after everything we talked about, I still didn't think I needed to fully share my story to get clients. I was pretty confident that customers would initially sign-up for class or fitness plans just because I was a Clover. This wasn't necessarily the most innovative plan but it made the most sense at a time when I was somewhat desperate; desperate to do exactly what I wanted, *how* I wanted.

✿✿✿

A few hours after thoroughly reviewing my business plan, I stood in my yard by the fountain and checked my watch once more. I waited for ten minutes before calling him. He said he wanted me to meet him outside in a few minutes, so I did. I was beginning to feel like my natural resistance to letting people in was slowly fading. I didn't like people in our business – and most people weren't just getting to know one Clover when they came into the picture. We were a package deal. I watched Saith roll out of the house with his phone to his ear when I was about to head inside.

"Took you long enough," I snapped.

"Sorry. I have something for you," Saith said, rolling to a complete stop by the fountain. "Come here."

I waited a minute before moving. "Don't be so pushy."

He snickered. I turned and looked up at the top window of his house. I swore I saw the curtain move. I turned back to Saith just as he pulled out a magazine. It was the latest issue of *Self*. He opened it to a page that was marked with a sticky note.

"If you tell anyone about this, I swear, I'll never talk to you again," he blurted. I smirked, but when I looked at him, he wasn't smiling. I nodded slowly. "There's this story in here about a trainer helping a paralytic athlete overcome paralysis with a set of exercises. You know, daily things that she'd make him do to keep him moving."

I grabbed the magazine from his hand. Somehow, I must've passed over that article. I glanced over it quickly. My eyes froze on the picture. She was white. He was black. She was holding his arm, and he was bending it like he was trying to make a muscle. I looked again. My eyes widened.

"Is that a prosthetic leg?" I blinked a few times. "Wait, so the trainer has a prosthetic leg?"

He nodded. "She lost it in Afghanistan. I think it's cool that she was able to become a fitness trainer despite not looking like a normal fitness trainer."

I cut my eyes at him. "What does a *normal* fitness trainer look like?"

He sighed. "Stop being so damn sensitive. You know what I mean. To the world, she doesn't fit the vision of the typical trainer."

I felt my face growing hot. I looked back down at the article. *You've got to stay on top of your stuff.* I wouldn't admit it to Saith, but as much as I loved fitness, my doubts were stronger at this point. I'd gone from reading health magazines cover to cover to literally, skimming them, more engrossed in the pictures than the words. *Get it together. This is who you are.*

"So, you think you can help me?"

Saith's deep voice broke me out of my thoughts. We'd talked about it. I wasn't so sure how it would work. After my father and I talked, I'd had some time to think. This would put more stress on my body, and I didn't really need that right now. More importantly, I didn't want to give Saith any idea that'd we would be able to be together. Wait. Where did that come from?

"Uh, well, I have to give it some thought," I said. "A prosthetic leg is different from a lifelong illness."

His eyes softened. "I get that. But, I think it could be good for both of us. Even if it's once a week." He looked down. "The crazy thing is, I doubt it'll make a difference for me either way."

My stomach dropped. Saith sounded defeated. I was about to agree to help him a few days a week when I heard someone walking up. I turned around, and his father was standing behind me.

"Saith, you didn't hear your phone?" he said, smiling at me. "Hi, Brelyn."

"Hi, Mr. Richards. How are you?"

"Good." He stood in front of Saith. "Dinner will be ready soon. Let's go."

I looked around. Why was I feeling like a guest in my own courtyard? I cleared my throat.

"Uh, I'll catch you later, Saith," I said, sliding off the fountain's edge to head inside. "We'll talk."

Saith's nostrils flared, and he gripped the wheels of his chair tightly. From the look of his knuckles, I could immediately tell he was upset.

"I'll call you after I eat," he said. He never looked at me or turned back around. He just rolled toward his house with his father following behind him.

❈ ❈ ❈

I was lying on my bed checking my social media feed. *Twitter* had just started to allow 300 characters instead of 140, which to be honest, was still too much for my generation's attention span. But for fitness ideas and things I wanted to say that required a little more, it was perfect. I was following back the last twenty people who followed me, something I did just to keep the flow of Bodies by Brelyn going and to interact with people. The last person that followed me was *EdunKis*. I followed back and smiled when I saw the avatar. She was an Indian girl with short black hair. I liked the way she decided to spell 'Eden,' replacing the 'e' with a 'u.'

I tweeted out a few tips to my followers about the small steps they could take to start eating healthier. Smiling, I typed: *Breakfast. Eat a bowl of oatmeal. And drink water. Don't feel rushed to eat healthy all at once. Start small.* I got excited just thinking about the retweets and messages I might receive. It was weird. One minute I felt like I was on top of the world, especially when I was working on fitness and health goals. The next I felt like an old lady with arthritis and who could barely do anything fitness related. Just before I put my tablet to sleep, I saw a notification. I smiled as I began reading it: *I started with oatmeal and eggs. I still use cheese though.* I replied: *No worries. Try egg whites next time.* ☺

Smiling, I hit the button on my tablet to put it to sleep. *Ding.* A new notification popped up. I scrolled through. It was a new DM from *EdunKis.* I smiled. A lot of my followers were teens just like me. I clicked on her bio again before reading her message. *16. Lover of all things fashion. Team #Kimye all day.* I giggled and opened the message.

It read: *Hey, Brelyn. Thanks for the follow. Your avi is cute. Keep in touch!*

I wrote back: *Thanks, Edun. I love yours too. I hope you like my fitness tips. New website coming soon.*

In my bio, I had already placed the Bodies by Brelyn website link. Right now, when you went to the site, it was just a landing page with all of my info, email, social media links and the 800 number we set up for the business. Under that, it said, site under construction. I'd been doing the work – outlining how I wanted it to look, working out the kinks of the app I wanted to create and lining up articles that would be sent out with the blog. Everything had to be perfect. I took off my Clover necklace and smiled. The moonlight was shining through my window, and the way it glistened made me warm inside.

Chapter 7

When I woke up the next day, I could already tell it wasn't going to be a good one. The pain in my lower back was horrible – nothing that an icy hot patch would help. The pain spoke to me before I even opened my eyes. It was clearly telling me to sit back and relax. School would have to wait. Getting up to pray with my family would have to wait. Checking my social media pages would have to wait. I reached for my Bodies by Brelyn notebook, happy that I'd left it right on my nightstand. My tablet was there also. I could get some work done without moving a lot. That was the only thing that couldn't wait. I grabbed my necklace and put it on, fingering the clover as I booted up my tablet.

I hated when the pain hit on a weekday because it usually meant that school would be put off for at least two days, if not the rest of the week. To say this was crazy would be an understatement. For one, it had gotten worse in the past month, and I hadn't even been able to work out. When I *was* working out, I was still able to do what I needed to do without feeling like my body was going to cave in under me. But, my parents insisted on me taking a break because they felt like the pressure was too much on my body. The doctor said light cardio would help. I didn't believe in *light* anything in the gym. I picked up my first dumbbell at seven.

I remember that day like it was yesterday. I told my father that I would out lift him. He held the fifty-pound weights, and I held the two-pound ones. My arms were hurting, but when he reached ten, I was still going. He looked at me and laughed. Mama came out yelling about her baby lifting weights, but Papa saw something. "She did ten reps," he had said. "I can't believe it."

"What's a rep?" I asked him. And that was when it started. I would work out with Mama when she did those crappy exercise videos. Whenever Emé went running in the summer, I ran a block with her, then stopped to get an ice cream cone. I guess it was in middle school that I finally realized fitness was what I loved. I found myself competing with the boys in school more than I jumped rope with the girls.

In fact, Desmond and I spent more time together at lunch when I was in sixth grade than Cashmere and me. While she was looking through *Glamour*, I was looking through *Fitness for Women*. Desmond would shoot hoops, and I'd use it as practice time to work on strengthening my arms. The rope jumping came in handy, too. Whenever Cashmere and her girls played double-dutch, I would play just so I could work my legs. I would yell "faster, faster" and speed jump as fast as they could turn. When it was my turn to turn the rope, I would make them go fast – but Cashmere would yell I was ruining the game. To her, it was about holding down your boobs and jumping cute, so guys would come over and mess with you. To this day, I didn't get it. Wasn't jumping rope just jumping rope?

For as long as I could remember, fitness had been my go-to for working out problems at school, home or anything that was bothering me. But it wasn't about relieving stress for me as much as it was about knowing I had a passion burning on the inside that made me want to learn about the world of exercise. It had been stripped from me in some ways – maybe not completely, but I never knew when my body would decide to put me on my ass. So even with the doctors saying it was okay to work out and with me launching Bodies by Brelyn in the next couple of weeks, I had to understand one thing. My body was now in charge of my destiny. Period.

❀ ❀ ❀

A few weeks later when I walked into Saith's house, the smell of baked chicken filled my nostrils. I hadn't seen Myla yet, but I could smell her perfume as soon as I walked into the foyer. It smelled of flowers with a hint of tree bark. For the life of me, I couldn't understand why someone so young liked such an old smell. Saith and I had been hanging out at this point almost daily. Our personal training sessions were going well, and he was gaining some strength in his leg, but for the most part, nothing had changed. Neither one of us were expecting immediate results, but the movement was a start. We were careful to keep our workouts a secret the first week, but Myla caught us one night. Since then, we let her hang out for the sessions just to keep her quiet.

"Hey, Brelyn," she said, flying down the steps. She hugged me tight as soon as she landed at the bottom. Mr. Richards was right behind her.

"Hi, Breyln. How's everything?"

Saith rolled next to me. "Dad, I think the chicken's been in long enough."

Mr. Richards turned to look in the kitchen. He ran his fingers over his head. Myla headed toward the kitchen before he could move.

"I got it, Unc," she said without looking at him.

"I'm good, Mr. Richards," I said, smiling at him.

His smile returned. "How are you doing?"

"Well, the magazine just hired a new editor in chief, so that's been keeping me busy. Otherwise, all is well."

I felt Saith's hand on mine. "Let's go sit down," he said.

Mr. Richards never looked Saith in his eyes the entire time we were standing there. Their silence toward each other was odd, but I didn't say anything. It was none of my business. I started heading to the kitchen. I'd only taken a few steps when I noticed Saith wasn't behind me. I turned back around. Saith was looking at his father. After a few minutes, he started moving toward me. I waited for him to reach me before saying anything.

"Did I come at a bad time?" I asked, watching Mr. Richards walk around us and into their large kitchen. The layout of their house was similar to ours; however, as expected it was decorated differently. I watched as Myla set the table for four and moved around the kitchen like she'd been doing it all her life. She occasionally looked over at me with a nervous grin.

"Bre, I told my father that you were helping me a little," Saith said, breaking me out of my concentration. I noticed how he disregarded my question.

I turned my head to him. "I thought we weren't talking much about that," I said, without being too obvious. I glanced over at Mr. Richards, who was obviously in his own world already. His cell phone was in his hand, and he was mumbling to himself. I put my finger to my lip, hushing Saith. I walked over and sat down at the table. Saith rolled up next to me.

"It's not like he's paying attention," he whispered, then continued into the larger part of the kitchen to help Myla.

I watched as he put a tossed salad on his lap and came back over to the table. I got up to help, but he pushed me gently back down.

"You're a guest," Mr. Richards voice chimed in.

I smiled at him weakly. His phone was now lying next to his empty plate. When Myla placed shrimp pasta down in front of me, my stomach rumbled. Saith promised I would love Myla's shrimp appetizer and his dad's chicken, so I hadn't eaten anything since lunch. I was ready to dig in.

"So, Bre," Myla said.

"Brelyn," I corrected, interrupting her. Bre was reserved for close friends and family.

"Right, sorry about that," she said. "What kind of exercises should Saith be doing at home to help him get his feeling back quicker?"

I stayed quiet. Either I wasn't outside the day we all agreed to keep this between us, or both Saith and Myla were setting me up.

"He saw us," Saith said.

Somehow, that still didn't ease my concern, but if we were seen, there was nothing that could be done about it.

"I don't understand why it's such a big secret," Mr. Richards said, grabbing a piece of bread. "But Saith made me promise not to tell your family or anyone else for that matter."

I winked at Saith. He was gaining more cool points in my book. "Well, it's just the whole girl, guy thing. Nothing major. They're very overprotective."

"So I heard," he said, without looking at me.

I felt my face tighten at his comment. I wasn't sure what he'd meant by that, but I was switching gears immediately.

"Myla, how are you adjusting to school?"

"It's okay. A little stuffy, but it's cool."

"Stuffy? You mean a bunch of rich kids all in the same place, doing the same thing, driving the same cars, kind of stuffy?"

She looked at me with a mouthful of food. "Well, sort of."

Saith grabbed more salad. I hadn't even seen him eat the first one. "Myla, Dad drops us off in a Hummer. We fit right in."

She chuckled. "I guess we do.

We continued eating in silence. I thought my family was weird for talking *too* much at dinner sometimes. But this was awkward. Silence beyond anything I could imagine.

"So, Saith tells me you're putting Johnson Mason on the cover for next month?" I said to Mr. Richards. He was a major real estate guru.

His eyes lit up. "Yes. Yes. I'm excited to have him be a part of the brand this year. He's going to be working on some other facets of Urban Central after we release the cover. Things I can't reveal quite yet, but it's going to be great."

Saith looked at me and smiled. I winked, catching myself from getting too giggly when I felt Myla staring at me. I stared at her but didn't say anything. This girl gave me the creeps sometimes. Her stare could quiet a marching band.

"Myla, Saith told me you have Mrs. Lewis for math. I had her in ninth grade as well."

"She's not that bad, just long winded and always giving too much homework," she said, fiddling with her earring. "But I like her."

"She said by the third assignment she had a pretty good handle on her routine," Mr. Richards chimed in.

I nodded and smiled. Saith reached his hand under the table and lightly touched the one that had fallen in my lap. I was finished eating.

"Do you want more?" Myla asked, interrupting the moment.

"Yeah, I do," I said. I turned to Saith. "Can you put some chicken on my plate? Myla, can you pass me the salad please?"

I knew she was extremely protective of Saith, that part was clear, but there was something else there. I wanted more than anything to not concern myself with what it was, but I couldn't ignore it. Then I looked down at her arm as it sat on the table. There was a scar. I'd never noticed it before, but I don't see how I could've missed it. It looked like it extended from her wrist to her elbow. I guess she noticed me staring because she quickly pulled her arm off the table.

"From the car accident," she said, continuing to stuff her face.

Mr. Richards cleared his throat. "Myla, why don't you start putting some of the food away since we're all done with the appetizer. I grabbed an apple pie and ice cream for dessert. You can pull that out, too, please. Brelyn, are you good?"

I nodded. "Yes, sir."

"I'm good," Saith said under his breath before continuing. "I'll help Myla."

"No, no son. Sit with your company. Have fun."

Mr. Richards got up from the table, and Myla followed slowly behind. Saith backed up from the table and looked at me. When I caught his eye, he had an empty look in them. I stood up and followed him to their back courtyard. When we were out of earshot, I turned to him.

"*The* car accident? Myla was in the car?" I blurted out.

He didn't say anything for a few minutes. "She was in the backseat when it happened."

I gasped. "I'm really sorry to hear that. Wow."

He was silent.

"How is she taking everything?"

His jaw flinched. Even with the moonlight casting a glow, I could see it.

"So I figured out a way to do those arm lifts you showed me without putting too much pressure on my back." He slowly raised both his arms and started to demonstrate. "With the weights of course."

He laughed. I didn't. My curiosity had been peaked. The uncomfortable feeling I'd been getting whenever I was around Myla probably had more to do with Saith than me. He was brushing it off like it was nothing.

"Glad to see the progress," I said, grabbing my phone to check the time. "I'll be heading home soon."

There was an awkwardness hanging over us that I couldn't explain. I wouldn't take it personally, but if he didn't want to talk, it was okay. He placed his hands back on the wheels of his chair and gently rolled forward.

"We can talk and walk," he said.

Once we made it to the front of the house, Saith stopped.

"I didn't mean for you to feel that way at dinner," he said. "I know my family is weird."

I looked at him. When I caught the smile, I laughed. "Everybody's family is weird."

I waited. Nothing.

"Listen, Saith," I continued. "You don't have to share anything personal with me, but I would like to at least know that I'm not crazy for thinking your cousin doesn't like me. I mean, I get it. I don't like all of Desmond's girlfriends."

He laughed. "How many does he have?"

"I meant when he has one."

I was staring off at the water fountain in front of my house. We'd be there shortly.

"What will we work on the next time you train me?" he asked.

"Some leg stuff. Simple."

I wasn't looking at him. He was staring at me, though. I could feel it.

"You mad at me?"

"About what?"

"Dinner."

"Why would I be mad at you? I would like some dessert, but you seemed just as ready to leave as I was."

He shrugged. "Never mind."

"Why don't you just say what you really want to say instead of asking me questions?"

His eyes narrowed. "What is it that you think I want to say?"

I crossed my arms. *I'm not going to argue with him.*

"If you have something to ask, then ask," he said.

I dropped my arms. "I just don't understand why you couldn't tell me Myla was in the car, too."

"I didn't tell you I was the one driving either."

Chapter 8

I stood frozen in place by Saith's confession. The chills running up my spine were evidence that I'd indeed heard him correctly. The faraway look on his face was another indicator that he'd definitely said what I thought. He was no longer facing me, but looking in the opposite direction. I saw the glassy look in the corner of his eyes. It reminded me of what my dad looked like when he was in deep thought or hurting about something. I'd dealt with some heavy blows in the last year. My heart almost dropped out of my chest when the doctors gave me my diagnosis. At this moment, I was experiencing something very close to that.

I don't know what I would do or say if I had been the cause of my own mother's death. Yet, Saith was sitting here bearing that news to someone he hadn't known that long. Sometimes I was hesitant to share everything I felt with my siblings for the sake of appearing strong – and they were my siblings. I had no idea what to do with this information. He trusted me with it, but I couldn't even bring myself to speak.

"Brelyn," he continued, bringing me out of my thoughts. "I was driving."

I swallowed before answering. "I heard you the first time. I just don't know what to say. Why did you tell me?" As soon as it left my mouth, I felt bad. "I didn't mean why like that. I just feel horrible and...and I don't know what to say. Sorry."

I was babbling, but I had nothing else to give right now. Except for an ear.

"Do you want to talk more about it?" I asked as we reached the fountain. I sat down and crossed my legs, forgetting that it was almost time for me to go in.

"I'm not sure what made me say anything now," he said, still not looking at me. Then, he slowly turned his head in my direction. "I don't sleep much at night."

"Your father? Is that why he's so distant?"

He nodded. "Imagine how he feels knowing that I'm the reason his wife is no longer here."

"You say that like she's not your mother?"

"No, I just. I just feel like it's a lot deeper than most people realize. I will never get over that night."

He slowly inched closer to me, dropping his voice down some. I leaned forward.

"To this day, I wonder how everything went so wrong and what happened. The night we got in the car was a typical evening. I was tired; exhausted from my game. Mom was so excited that I'd scored twenty-three points. She'd even grabbed the ball after my winning shot when we were alone in the gymnasium after the game. I lifted her up a little as she attempted a three-pointer. It didn't go in, but I grabbed the ball for the rebound and handed it to her. She made it. So when we got to the car, I wanted to drive. I had my permit. There was no reason I couldn't drive. Mom was excited to let me. I was her growing baby, as she would say."

He paused and looked around. I didn't want to push him, but the story had me locked in.

"When I pulled into traffic, I was ready. I'd been practicing for years. My father would let me drive his truck in a large lot, just circles, weaving in and out of cones. Parallel parking until my hands were numb. I was ready. I could back up down a street in ten seconds without swerving once. I could even make the truck lean on two wheels, but my parents had never seen that and I never told them. I didn't know what I was getting into that night. My arm was around my mother's neck as we walked to the car. She held me around my waist. She kissed my cheek letting me know that I meant the world to her."

I could tell by the way he was letting it all out that he'd been holding it in for a while. How could he talk to his father or cousin about it? If he felt guilty, I'm sure they hadn't been making that easy. That explains her behavior. She blames him. She wanted to know if I knew.

He continued. "Myla wasn't able to go to my game, but she was right down the street at a friend's. We stopped to pick her up. I pulled back into traffic. A few blocks later, I pulled up at a stop sign. I saw the truck on the other side stop at his. Mom and I were singing and jamming to our favorite Earth, Wind and Fire song. Myla was texting someone. I *was* paying attention, and we had both stopped at our respective stop signs. We did. Full brakes."

My phone vibrated. Mom was checking on me. I knew without even looking down that it was her. When I'd asked to go over Saith's for dinner, I didn't get all into details. It was my first sit down with his family. My parents would surely want to have one soon enough.

"I'm sorry. My mom."

He looked up at the window. "If you have to go, I understand."

I gently touched his hand. "No way. Not now. Go ahead."

He sighed and blinked a few times. It had to be hard telling this story without breaking down crying. I didn't want to push. As I rubbed his hand, I noticed he relaxed a little.

"The other driver must've thought when I was waving my hand dancing, that I was giving him the right away. And he went at the same time I hit the gas. The impact immediately took my breath away. I felt my mother's body hit mine as we swerved and whirled into another car. I was stuck. She was dead. I couldn't really see Myla from the back, but I could hear her groaning. Once the ambulance arrived, the trip to the hospital only took us ten minutes, but it felt like forever. Then my dad showed up."

I was sweating just listening to him. When he mentioned hospital, I literally thought in that split second of the day I'd been rushed in. But I came out alive, glad that I had. There was a knot in my stomach thinking about how Saith couldn't say the same about his mother.

"When my dad got there, I could hear the screams. He was livid. But he didn't know I was driving. He screamed bloody murder for the truck driver's head. He yelled. He fussed. But then the nurse came out. My eyes were open. From my bed, I could see her attempting to calm him down. I could feel my heart racing as I waited for her to tell him what I knew because I'd felt her body hit mine. It was like my mother and I were one. The impact told me she was gone instantly. Somehow, my breath left my body at the same time she took her last one."

I assumed he was done. He was quiet. My phone vibrated again. I texted my mom back that I was coming in shortly. It was nine, but tomorrow was Friday. I'd be fine. Before Saith could say anything else, it was all making sense to me. His father's distance. Myla's disposition. Their awkward silence that spoke volumes to someone like me. I'd picked up on it, but I'd brushed it off as myself having a "Cashmere" moment – overthinking.

"My father's distance makes sense," Saith continued. I shuddered at the fact that what I'd been thinking he'd just said. "Isn't it something? I can't feel much movement, but I can feel his anger throughout my whole body whenever he's near me."

I had never been this speechless. It was scary to think that at a moment where he was feeling the most uncertain and vulnerable, he was sharing it with someone who couldn't help him. I stared at Saith for a few minutes and was about to speak when my front door opened. I looked over and frowned when I saw Papa.

"Baby girl," he said as he waved at Saith.

I stood up but didn't start walking. I only needed a few more minutes, but my father's looming shadow remained. I turned back to Saith, who at this point hadn't moved an inch. He slowly looked back up at me. How can I just walk away at a time like this? If there was ever a moment when I wanted to be outright rebellious, it was right now. I looked back over at the door. Papa was walking over to me slowly, hands in his bathrobe pockets.

"I'll FaceTime you," I said to Saith, lightly touching his shoulder. "I promise."

I bent down and kissed his cheek before I even realized what I was doing. Then I whispered in his ear, "It's not your fault. She's still with you."

I heard sighing behind me. Just as I turned around and Saith started rolling away, Mama came to the door.

"Brelyn Michele," she called. "Let's go, now."

Papa reached for my hand, but I grabbed him around the waist. He put his arm around my shoulder, and I fell into his tummy. He squeezed my shoulder as we entered the house. Mama had a stern look on her face, but she didn't say anything. As soon as my father locked the door, she kissed my cheek.

"I'm not trying to keep you from enjoying life," she said. "Just don't push it. We have a system in place for a reason."

My illness had us feeling like we had to walk on eggshells, yet there were moments when I ignored exactly what I was feeling. I wouldn't dwell on the idea of what I couldn't do. I focused on what I could. Somewhere in my fifteen-year-old body, I'd developed strong feelings for someone outside of my family. I could ignore them, but that wouldn't make any sense considering the person who they were for hadn't been able to ignore his.

Chapter 9

I was glad when Saturday finally arrived, and I could direct my focus to my business site. Getting my schoolwork submitted yesterday was somewhat of a challenge, but I had some fun with it. I used my website as an example for my business class. There were only three pages, but each page was easy to navigate and outlined everything anyone needed to know about Bodies By Brelyn. Information regarding the services offered was front and center. It showed that there were three small packages available to anyone who needed assistance, with several options to book a virtual training session. The internet was overwhelming when it came to information on nutrition and fitness, so when I questioned how I could position myself online, I chose to focus on one thing – thirty-minute workout sessions with a meal preparation plan attached.

Clients could receive coaching via email and Skype. I nervously chuckled as I typed my new bio. Being vulnerable about lupus was one thing in person, but to know whenever somebody clicked my website that they would re-read the same story again and again – that was creepy. I had no idea why I was making such a big deal out of it. I knew it was the key to my branding. I scrolled over to check my emails and noticed that someone was interested in one of my introductory packages. It was two hundred dollars and included five, thirty-minute workout sessions and a breakfast kick starter meal plan for the week. I smiled when I realized it was from EdunKis.

Hi Brelyn,

It's Paris. You remember me as EdunKis on Twitter. I'm glad to see your site up and running. I've struggled with my weight for the last two years and could use some help. I'm not sure if I can afford your packages, but I was wondering if we could email about it. Do you have anything custom for someone on a budget? Let me know how to precede from here.

Papa always said that if people could get you to change your prices, they would. However, I thought it was admirable of her to reach out and ask for help. I went back to Twitter to see her avatar. I noticed it was just her face. From the looks of it, she didn't look like she needed to lose a lot of weight, but I knew plenty of overweight people with thin faces. I had a cousin like that. The best I could do for her was a meal plan for eighty dollars, but I wasn't sure if that would help. I hated how I could be my own worst enemy at times. It was my own suppressing thoughts that talked me out of something before I even gave it a chance. I had to trust that I could do this.

I hit reply: *Hi Paris, Thanks so much for reaching out. I have a package option that may help you. It's just a three-day meal plan, but everything starts in the kitchen. What you put in your body is what matters at this point. If you're interested, an immediate payment of eighty dollars can be submitted to brelyn@bodiesbybrelyn.com via PayPal. Let me know if you have any questions. Best, Brelyn*

I didn't sit to wait for a reply. My parents taught me the true meaning of knowing your worth in business and letting people decide if they wanted to be a part of it. What little doubt that tried to creep in was immediately gone when my cell phone rang. I was getting used to seeing Saith's face pop up on the screen, and I liked the warm feelings that felt come over me when I did.

"Hey, you," I said, smiling.

"Hey, love," he replied. "What's up?"

Up until now, my father and brother had been the only two men in my life to use affectionate names with me. But, up until now, I hadn't let anyone else enter my world.

"Just emailed a potential client back."

"Really? That's cool. Who was it?"

"Somebody I met on Twitter."

I could hear him moving around.

"Are you nervous about that?"

I sat up. "About what?"

"Just working with people that you've never met before. I thought you were going to focus on your former clients only."

"Well, it's an online business. I'm not going to *not* work with others. It's only via Skype and email."

He was quiet. "Just be careful. You know how people are with the internet."

I stood up and started walking around. "It'll be okay. What are you doing today?"

"I was hoping we could hang out."

"Me too. Desmond and I are going to pick up some things for his prom, but I'll call you when I'm done. What's the plan?"

"You'll see," he said. I could hear the smile in his voice. "Call me when you're done."

"I will," I said, hanging up.

I hurried downstairs to find Desmond cooking.

"My favorite," I said, sniffing the air. I was glad it was a cheat day. Eating healthy was fun when it was my choice. I'd been going the extra mile with the lupus. I took in the buttermilk pancakes, with the butter dripping from the sides; the turkey bacon and grits, which I know my brother doused with sugar just for me; and the fresh squeezed orange juice. "Dang, bro. You went all out for your sis, huh?" I teased.

"Nope. I have someone coming over," he said. "But you're more than welcome to *a* pancake, *a* slice of bacon and *a* cup of OJ."

I playfully started crying. "What about the grits?"

"*A* bowl. And that's raw sugar, not white."

I walked over to him and hugged him. "What if I just knock everything off the table and see how long it'll take you to cook again for your lady friend?"

He laughed. "You would do me like that?" He started making plates.

"Take these to Mom and Dad. I'll have ours ready when you get back. Then, we can talk."

I could tell by the way he said it that it would be a long talk. I knew it had everything to do with Saith and I was ready. Desmond had his concerns, just like any big brother would, but my life was my own. As I carried the plates up to our parents, my phone chimed from inside my jacket pocket. I knew from the sound that it was an email from my website.

"Mama, Papa. It's me with breakfast," I called out. I couldn't open the door since my hands were full.

The door flew open. My mother grabbed the plates from me and kissed me on my cheek.

"Tell Desmond I'm going to kill him for making you carry these up," she said.

I flinched. "I'm not weak. It's just food."

I hugged her, then went inside their bedroom to hug my father. "Papa Bear," I teased.

He tickled me. "I love your chicken, Bre, but your brother has you beat with breakfast," he said, as my mother placed his plate down in front of him.

I playfully crossed my arms in a huff. "That sucks."

He chuckled. "Alright. Go on. Your mother and I are busy."

I already knew what busy meant, so I left without another word. I caught the way my mother looked at my father right before I left. Their love permeated throughout their bedroom. Heavy. I was wondering if that's the way I was feeling about Saith? Could it even be put into words? Once I made it back downstairs, Desmond had our food trays set up in the living room in front of the TV. I sat down and started digging in. Desmond stopped me.

"Thank you God, for this food we're receiving for the nourishment of our souls. Amen."

"Amen," I said, already with a mouthful. "I wanted to make sure I get my seconds before your friend gets here. What's her name again?"

He nudged me. "Let's talk about a name we both know."

I continued to chew. "Saith," I said, without missing a beat.

"What's going on with you two?"

"Probably the same thing that's going on between you and your friend."

I looked at Desmond. He had that same vein that popped out the side of his head that my father had whenever he got annoyed. His was twitching. Good. He's not mad. Yet.

"Bre," he started. "Don't do that. I'm just asking."

"And I'm just telling you. If you think you're going to scare me into leaving Saith alone, you're wrong."

"I don't need to scare you; I can just scare him. And trust me," he said, sipping his juice. "It'll work."

I put my fork down. Tears sprang to my eyes. "What's the big deal?"

"You see how Cashmere's running around here acting crazy. Do I really need to answer that question?"

"You do if you want me to even consider what you have to say because I'm *not* Cashmere."

He glared at me. Then, his face softened. He grabbed my chin and looked me in my eyes. "What do I do if you get carried away like she has? How do I tell Dad I failed?"

I sighed. My brother's love for the women in his family was unmatched. My father was a true protector, but my brother saw the layers underneath us all because he spent time with each one of us on a regular basis. He knew what was bothering anyone of us at any given time, with almost no words. I snatched my chin out of his grip.

"You're not, Dad. When will you get that through your head, Des," I said. "I know you love us, but you aren't our father."

He turned back to his plate. "I wasn't trying to be, but I am your big brother."

"And I love you," I said, touching his arm. "I don't like when you compare Cashmere and me. It isn't fair to me."

Tears were now streaming down my face. "I like Saith. He likes me. Big deal."

"He's a year older than you."

"You dated Laura. She's a year younger than you."

He took a bite of his pancakes and slowly swallowed. "I did. And to be honest, I wish I hadn't."

"A year isn't that bad, Des. Girls mature quicker than guys."

He looked at me again, his plate now empty. "My fear exactly."

My eyes widened. I realized what Desmond was thinking. The change in our culture had shifted. Girls were now making moves on guys before guys could even figure out whether he'd hit puberty or not. Social media glamorized girls being more interested in sex and body image than anything else. I heard girls at my school or at the mall always brag about the *moves* they made on guys and how many numbers they got.

"Desmond, I wouldn't have sex with Saith," I said, whispering.

"Doesn't mean he wouldn't have sex with you."

I made a face. "Uh, so, not sure if you noticed but, he's not really equipped to handle that kind of thing."

He turned his head toward me. The smile was coming back.

"Bre, stop. I'm serious," he continued. "We've seen movies where people can get around their disability."

"I know, but can you just trust that I'll make the right decisions? The more you push, the more I'll pull," I said. I was half joking. "I'm just making a point, not saying I'll do anything. Cashmere may be tripping right now, but it's the hold that our parents have on us. Sometimes, we just want to be an individual. Not a Clover."

We stood up, plates in hand and headed back to the kitchen. I helped Desmond put the rest of the food away and clean up. We were both silent, but I knew it was because we were thinking. There was one thing I noticed that I had to appreciate about my brother. It made me happy to know that no matter how protective he was he treated me like I was human. I watched him as we headed to the garage. I stopped him.

"Hey, Des," I said, walking over to him. I jumped up a little to kiss his cheek. "Thank you for seeing me."

He scrunched his face. As he realized what I meant, he started smiling. He pulled me into his arms. "I always do, kiddo."

Chapter 10

"I never meant to make you feel like that," Saith said.

I watched him as he moved around, trying to do an arm exercise I'd given him. I was working on my computer but had my FaceTime chat up. He was in his room lifting a medicine ball over his head, stopping in between breaths to talk to me. I giggled as he made silly faces, faking how heavy the ball was.

"Bre, I can't lift – it anymore," he said, huffing and puffing. I rolled my eyes.

"Yeah, yeah. So, where are your folks?"

We hadn't said much about the night he'd told me he was driving the car that killed his mother. It was as if he'd gotten off his chest to someone outside his family and that was all he'd needed.

"Dad took Myla to the store to grab some things for an art class she wants to take."

"An art class? Where?" I said, tapping away at the keys.

"At Mighty Writer's Arts Center," he said. "You know of it?"

"Yeah. I love that place. Mom and Dad used to make us go every summer."

"You guys don't go anymore?"

"With all that we do, no. No time. But I got a good four years out of that program. It's pretty good."

"Yeah. She's going to the one downtown, on Market street."

"Did you know about the other locations? There's one up this way."

I paused when I saw an eighty dollar payment from a Paypal email address that I didn't recognize. *Paris.Rivers@gmail.com.* I smiled when I realized who it was from. EdunKis, I thought. I always had to associate her screen name with her real name. It was exciting getting my first paying client after having to physically shut down my exercise classes. I thought I would never see the so-called rainbow that my mother kept saying showed up after the storm. I emailed her back.

Thank you for your prompt payment. In two business days, after you complete the attached questionnaire, you will receive a simple breakfast nutrition plan and a low-impact workout, as per the Brelyn Beginner's Kit plan that you have chosen. I look forward to helping you be your best self. Brelyn M. Clover

"You want to get back to me?" Saith asked.

I'd completely forgotten we had been FaceTiming. I looked at the time. It was almost three in the afternoon. Sunday's always seemed to rush by me when I was getting the most work done.

"Sorry," I said. "We're about to have some family time, so I have to go anyway. We'll chat afterward?"

He pouted, then smiled. "Okay. I gotta get my homework done. Call me later."

He abruptly ended the call. I stared at the screen for a minute, then stood up. I couldn't wait to tell Papa that I'd signed on my first official client. A part of me wanted to wait, because I knew Mama would ask a lot of questions. I knew no matter what I did, she'd find a way to bring up how I needed to be extra careful. She would probably warn me about sending so many emails in my condition. Papa would give me the reassurance I needed. For now, it was our monthly meeting time, and I wanted to put everything on the table. Cashmere came bursting into my room just as I stood up.

"Time for the Clover Circle," she said. I noticed she had rollers in her head. "You feeling okay?"

"Yep. Coming now," I frowned. "Why do you have rollers in your hair? That defeated the purpose of going to the salon yesterday."

She came over and stood in front of my mirror. She took one of the rollers out, and I watched as her hair flowed off the roller and bounced back in place. I clapped.

"I love it," I said, walking over and pulling the curl. "She did a roller set?"

Cashmere nodded. "Yes, and the product she used will help keep my hair in place. I don't have to wrap it and put the rollers in every night. I didn't want to lay on it last night."

"Good stuff," I said, wrapping my arm around her neck. She squinted and threw her arm around my waist. She kissed my cheek.

"Time for you to do something to that wig on your head, sis."

She dodged out the way before I could hit her. I chased her out my room all the way downstairs. When we got there, Emé was standing there. She had a guy with her that I'd never seen before. Cashmere and I both stopped moving. My mouth was open, but nothing came out. Before either of us could say or ask anything, Emé came over and hugged us.

"What's up, babies? How's it going here at the Clover castle?"

I put on a smile. "Hey, sissy. Who's your friend?"

She turned and looked at him, then waved him over. "This is Derrick. He'll be working at the DermaSpa with Noni."

Cashmere waved at him, but her face said everything I was thinking. She tilted her head side to side, then moved forward to shake his hand.

"I'm Cashmere, nice to meet you," she said, shaking his hand. She turned around and moved past me to head to the kitchen. "I'll grab the lemonade."

"Nice to meet you," he said. "And you must be Brelyn?"

My smile was wavering, but I tried to keep it on. "I am. What's up?"

Emé's hand was still on my shoulder. "So, how's your body been treating you?" she whispered, out of Derrick's earshot.

"Like it does every day," I said through clenched teeth. "Like gold."

She pinched me, then winked. "I'm just concerned."

"Not in front of company. You shouldn't be," I said, faking an English accent. I wrapped my arm around her waist. "Love you, though."

Our parents came walking down the stairs with Desmond following behind them. Cashmere came out the kitchen with the tray of lemonade and six glasses. I chuckled. My sister understood what didn't need to be spoken.

"Papa," Emé said, walking over to him. He embraced her just like he always did – like she was his firstborn. My father's beaming face and his protruding chest said it all.

"Hey, baby girl." He kissed both her cheeks and walked over to Derrick.

"Desmond," he said. He extended his hand.

"Derrick," he responded, grabbing my father's hand firmly. "I was just dropping Emé off. I'll be back to get her in a few hours."

Papa smiled. "Well of course you were. I know my daughter wouldn't invite someone who wasn't family to a family meeting."

"Daddy," Emé seethed. Desmond laughed, while Cashmere and I chuckled.

"I'll take these in the living room," Cashmere said.

"Wait up, sis," Desmond called out, following behind her.

Mama walked over to Emé. "We'll have our girls' day this week."

Emé smiled and hugged her close with one arm. "Yes, two. We have to make up for last week."

I swallowed. Mom and Emé never missed their girls' day. I hadn't even noticed that my mother hadn't gone out with Emé last week. Something was definitely off.

"Okay, everybody. Let's go," Papa said. "Derrick, she should be done in two hours."

"I told him one," she said.

My father pinched his lips together. "Derrick, why don't you call her and see where we are?"

"No problem, sir. Emé," he said, walking over to her. "Spend some time with your family. We can push our plans back another hour. No big deal."

He kissed her softly on the cheek. "Nice meeting everybody," he said, letting himself out.

Either Emé was trying to piss my father off, or she had been out with Derrick earlier that day, and he *had* to drop her off. I grabbed my mother's hand and walked into the living room. Even with how large our foyer area was, I could hear the bellowing sound of his voice chewing Emé out for the stunt she pulled. My mother's firm hand grasped my neck gently. She kissed my forehead, and I fell into her bosom.

"I love you, Mama," I said, sitting down next to Desmond on the couch and throwing my feet up on his lap. He grabbed them and started rubbing and tickling them.

"Stop, Des," I joked.

Before he could respond, Papa and Emé walked into the living room. By the pinched look on her face, I knew my father had won whatever argument they'd had.

"Okay, Clovers," he said, putting his militant smile back on. "First, I love all of you."

Mama cleared her throat.

"My apologies," he said. "Roundup."

We all stood up and grabbed each other's hands. We bowed our heads.

"Precious Lord, we thank you for this day and for everything you've blessed us with. More important than all the businesses, the money or the fame, we appreciate family. Thank you for the joy you bless us with. The joy of knowing that no matter what the world thinks of us, You love us. You treasure us, and You will always love us. Help me be the best father I can be and the best husband. Lead me as I lead my family. Help me never to forget where my help comes from and help each person in this room continue to put You first so they can experience that profound love You give. In Jesus name, Amen."

"Amen," we all said in unison. As we sat back down, I noticed Emé's phone in her hand. I looked down at Mama's right hand. Emé had been standing next to my mother, on her right side, holding her phone in her left hand. That would mean they hadn't held hands during the prayer. I looked at

Papa to see if he'd seen it, but he just sat down as Cashmere poured everyone a glass of lemonade. Desmond tapped my shoulder as we headed back to the couch.

"I saw that," he whispered to me, kissing my cheek.

I looked at him and winked knowingly. We were always on the same page. I would've been surprised had he *not* caught it.

"Okay. So first things first. Does anybody have anything they want to get off their chest? About business matters, family or anything?"

Mama raised her hand like a little school girl Papa laughed. "Go ahead, Queen."

"Well, I have good news. Reese Pieces has been selected to be featured in O's magazine. Clara is working her butt off to get the word out about this new line," my mother said.

Clara was my mother's publicist. She always managed to get the best magazine placements for our businesses. People thought it was easy, just because of who we were, but we'd gotten more 'no's' than people could imagine.

"She has been doing great. Proud of you, babe," he said, rubbing Mama's hand. "Bre, how's everything with your new website? I love the new layout and the message," Papa said.

I beamed. "Thanks, Papa. Everything is fine. The first client paid this morning."

Emé walked over and sat next to Desmond and me. "You didn't tell me that, kiddo?"

I stopped smiling. "Emé, we haven't talked all week."

Everyone looked at Emé. "Emé, you haven't talked to your sister all week?"

Even Mama was shocked about that. There wasn't a day that went by without Emé and I talking. Even the days that I wanted nothing to do with a Clover, she found a way to get in

86

my heart and mind. I hadn't meant to say anything, but the front she was putting up was irritating me. She could pull it off with Mama, but not with me. Papa cleared his throat. Desmond put his phone down on his lap.

"Hey, big sis. I know we're younger than you, but is everything okay?" he said. "It's one thing to have some time where you don't speak to our parents, I mean we all have those days. And we live here. But you not talking to Brelyn is weird. Even for you."

I watched Papa sit back and relax against the chair as Desmond took over the meeting. I knew he was in no way offended. One thing about the Clover clan is we always respected each other's opinion, even if it wasn't asked for. We also didn't have this "superior" attitude with each other. Papa started the meetings, but anybody could speak at any time, as long as we waited until the other person was finished.

"I'm just tired; nothing new," she said.

"Then it wouldn't change your routine," Cashmere said. I looked at Cash. Papa looked at me. I shrugged.

"Listen, I'm not going to let everyone jump down my back about being tired. Opening a spa and doing rehearsals all day isn't easy," she continued. "It's just a journey that I have to embark on alone. Nothing major."

"Do you need help in the office? Maybe I could do some things from home when I'm not working on my business," Mama chimed in.

"Which is never," Emé quipped.

I'd had enough. If there was someone I was more protective of than Desmond, it was Mama.

"Damned if she do, damned if she don't," I said. "Don't take your frustration out on Mama because you can't keep your ducks in a row. She offered to help."

Desmond grabbed my shoulder and pushed me back against the couch. "Sis, don't upset yourself."

I shook my shoulder out of his grasp. "I'm not a baby. Emé's acting like we all did something to her."

"Brelyn," Papa said. "That's enough."

By now, tears brimmed my eyes. If I was going to end up crying, I was going to get some mileage out of it. "You live on your own, so I don't expect to see you every day, but when you do come, you walk around like somebody did something to you."

"Bre, are you mad because she doesn't talk to you every day like she used to? If you are, just tell her? Emé, is there a reason you don't call every day like before?"

I cut my eyes at Cashmere. "No. She's just having a fit about something none of us know about, and she wants us to kiss her ass until she's ready to tell us."

I was breathing heavy at this point. Mama looked at me with a sadness I couldn't explain. She just shook her head and stood up.

"Brelyn, it's okay," she said. "Just let it go."

Emé hadn't said a word since I started. She glared at me. Desmond pulled me back into his arms. "It's okay, baby girl. Relax," he said.

I didn't even realize I was breathing heavily until I felt my heart beating against my own chest.

Papa stood up. "I let you have your moment because I understand you're hurt," he said, staring at me. "But cursing in front of your parents shouldn't even be something you're comfortable with. Get it right. Now."

I looked at him, then at Mama. I looked down. "I'm sorry."

"For what?" Papa continued.

"I apologize for disrespecting you and Mama." I looked at Emé. "And Emé."

She didn't say anything, but Mama did. "I forgive you, Brelyn."

Papa nodded. He turned back to Emé. "Emé, you're grown; I can't tell you what to say or how to say it. But you're not leaving here until we know you're okay. That's all we care about."

Emé looked around at everyone. She hadn't moved since the conversation started. The only thing that spoke were her eyes. Her gaze bounced from each one of us several times before she opened her mouth.

"It's funny, Dad. You always used to remember, even Mom remembered. For the last two years, I didn't say anything. I just chose to deal with it alone. I decided it wasn't worth causing any friction in your marriage."

Mama gasped. "Emé, I'm so sorry. We honestly forgot."

Emé snapped her head in Mama's direction. "You see. That's the thing. I will *never* forget."

The rest of us sat frozen in place. We were clueless. Then, it hit me. *Emé's mother.* It had to have something to do with her. That's the only thing that they could've been talking about. It was a piece of Emé's life that we didn't really know much about. We'd all been born into a situation that had already started before we came along. I still couldn't bring myself to say anything. Desmond squeezed my hand.

"Emé, do you want us to step out while you talk to Mom and Dad?" he asked.

"No," she said. "You're fine. I've just learned that it's something I have to deal with on my own."

She stood up abruptly, dropping her purse and phone to the floor. Cashmere bent down to pick it up. I knew the situation was deep when Cashmere couldn't even think of a question to ask. She hadn't said anything since my outburst.

"Emé, you know I could never forget your mother. It's been twenty-something years."

"It's been twenty-two to be exact."

Papa swallowed, and Mama cleared her throat. They both didn't have much to say. Desmond grabbed my hand and Cashmere's.

"We'll be in my room," he said, pulling us back toward the foyer. I was pulling against his hand. I didn't want to go, but I knew Emé wouldn't say much with all of us there. It was a dark part of her life that we knew only the basics about. Her mother had passed when she was six from cancer. Two years later, our parents married. That was it. We didn't know much of anything else. The details had always been a secret. Desmond and Cashmere stopped on the bottom step as I pulled my hand away.

"You okay?" he asked.

"I'm fine," I said, looking toward the kitchen. "I need my water bottle."

I was lucky I'd left it in the refrigerator earlier that day. I had to have a lot of water. They both knew that.

"I can grab it for you," he said as Cashmere ascended up the stairs.

"No," I snapped. "I'm not handicapped."

He stared at me for a second, then continued behind Cashmere without another word.

I waited until they were no longer in sight. I walked to the kitchen to get my water bottle. A few minutes later, I crept slowly past the living room. I wasn't sure what I would catch, but I hadn't expected to catch what I did.

"Dad, please. You couldn't wait to move on," I heard Emé say. "You think I don't know you were seeing her long before Mom died."

I clasped my hand to my mouth and waited for my heart to stop racing. When I was sure they hadn't heard me, I continued toward the steps, taking them two at a time to get back to my safe haven.

Chapter 11

I'd only sat in Desmond's room for an hour. I started feeling more fatigued and went to lay down in my own room. Just when I'd gotten into a deep sleep, Mama called us downstairs to eat. The first thing I noticed when I took my seat at the dining room table was that Emé wasn't there. Neither was Papa. I didn't say anything until everyone else was settled at the table and Mama put the chicken out.

"So they're skipping out?" I asked.

Desmond and Cashmere continued to dip their food like it was the norm for our head of the table to be empty.

"Brelyn, baby, everyone needs a break. I'll bless the food," Mama said with a strained voice.

I didn't even have time to close my eyes. The prayer was quick. Mama started digging in, passing the mashed potatoes to Cashmere and me with no regards to the fact that she had to skip over a seat where Emé would've been sitting. She looked over at me and paused. Her stern look said it all.

"Eat. Now."

So I did, but I barely enjoyed it. I'd been feeling crazy for the past couple of days – my body had been going in and out of a state of pain. I wasn't going to make a huge deal about it, but if by the third day the medicine wasn't working, I would have to tell Mama. I wouldn't be going back to school until Wednesday, so I had a lot of work to get done. That and my website would be my focus for the next few days. I'd already missed enough action in school. I didn't want to say anything and have Mama keep me out for the week.

"Brelyn, how are your assignments coming along?" she asked. Her intuition was definitely strong.

"Good, I submitted everything before we came down for the meeting."

She winked at me. "I was able to see the grades for the last few weeks. Keep up the good work. Maybe we'll go shopping this weekend?"

"With Emé?"

She looked at me and swallowed the rest of the wine she was drinking. She looked at Cashmere and then at Desmond. He just kept eating.

"We haven't had a lot of us time lately. Just you and me."

For the next hour, I didn't say anything else. Annoyed would be an understatement. I didn't need to be reminded that I was the baby of the family. I knew; and so did they. But whatever they thought they were protecting me from was a lie. I'd find out one way or the other what was going on. Somehow I felt it was the one thing that would help me understand my family better. If I wasn't struggling with pain, I was struggling with the constant battle of wondering if I really fit in with my family or not. They didn't make that easy with moments like this. But I would get to the bottom of it.

❧ ❧ ❧

Later that night, I crept into Cashmere's room to see what she was doing. I knew even she wouldn't be sleep. She should've been, but my instincts were always right. She was on the phone when I knocked on the door. I could hear her arguing with someone.

"What's up?" she called out.

"It's me, sissy," I said.

"I'll call you back," I heard her say. Ten seconds later, the door popped open.

I walked in and sat down on her bed. "You still up, huh?"

"Yeah; trying to sort out some things," she said, throwing her phone on the bed. She laid her head on my lap and got comfortable. "Crazy shit with Emé, right?"

"Crazy is an understatement," I said. "When did all of this start? Earlier this year everything seemed to be going well."

"Bre, our parents don't tell us a lot, but I pick up on everything," she continued. "I have no idea why it's such a big secret."

"Why what is such a big secret?"

She sighed. "Listen, you will not get me in trouble with Mama and Papa."

I pushed her head off my lap. "Then why say something in the first place?"

She shrugged. "You and Mama are close? How do I know you don't already know?"

I squinted at my sister. She was fishing, and I would not take the bait. This imaginary idea that Cashmere had that Mama loved me more than her was just that – imaginary.

"Whatever, Cash," I said, walking to the door. "I only came in here to talk to you. I'm not up for the back and forth."

She threw her hands up and walked over to her mirror. "Brelyn, there will always be some kind of back and forth. Your innocence gets the best of you."

"What is that supposed to mean?"

"You see the good in everybody. Even Desmond and I could tell Emé was tripping tonight. We left it alone. In your mind, every piece is supposed to fit perfectly. And that's the part you get from Daddy."

She started rolling her hair. Her phone rang, and she grabbed it in a huff. "I said I'll call you back," she said, hanging up.

I was standing with my arms crossed waiting for her to finish what she was saying. I was seething inside, but curiosity made me bite my tongue.

"I'm a positive person. Nothing wrong with that."

She looked at me and rolled her eyes. "Girl, you're sweet as pie, and that's the bottom line. You have Mama's nurturing ways and Papa's feisty passion. It works."

"You seem to think there's something wrong with it, so it can't be working?"

I had other things I wanted to say, such as how Cashmere's head was so far down in the boy's lap that she was dating she wouldn't know anything about how I'd grown in the last six months. But I knew she was close to saying something about the *secret* I had no idea about. She put her brush down. Frustrated, she turned back to me with a hand on her hip.

"Okay, Bre. So, you mean to tell me you never, *ever* picked up on how close you and Emé are? How she takes you out all the time, tells you grown woman secrets that she probably doesn't even tell, Mama?"

I put a finger to my lip when I heard a noise coming from the hallway. Desmond's bedroom was upstairs, and he had a kitchen on his level. Cashmere walked over and cracked her door.

"It's Papa," she whispered. After a few minutes, she closed the door. "He's back in his office. I heard the door shut."

Our father's office door had a more distinct sound than other doors in our house. It was the heaviest and the most expensive. Cashmere turned her attention back to me.

"Since you're so nosy, how are you and Saith doing?"

I smiled. "I haven't talked to him since before dinner, but we texted. He's already in bed."

She nodded, interested. "So, would you have sex with him?"

I frowned. "Cash, I'm not ready for that. I take it you've had it more than either of us could probably count," I teased. I wanted her to stay focused.

"I wouldn't be with Robbie if I weren't ready for it," she said. "Either way, I had to get ready."

I noticed how her voice dropped a few octaves. Her confidence had slipped that quickly. Cash had a firm conviction and air about her when she spoke, so when she didn't, I picked up on it immediately. I'd noticed it wasn't there the last few times she discussed Robbie.

"So, what does that have to do with my innocence and Emé?"

She finished rolling up her hair and walked back to me. She lightly grabbed my arms and stared me in the face. She waited a few minutes. Then, she spoke.

"Brelyn Michele Clover, what I'm about to tell you must never leave this room. I don't care what happens, you better take this to your grave. I won't care about your sickness if you do say something. I'll kick your little butt."

I smirked. Cashmere would; I knew it. But I'd beaten her up twice growing up. She had another thing coming if she thought my sickness would give her a one up on me. I was more offended that she thought I would even say anything. I was Mama's baby for sure, but nothing my siblings had ever shared with me left my mouth. Mama just had ways that made them tell her what she needed to know.

"Pinky swear," I said, for old times sake. I stuck out my pinky. My sister locked hers with mine and pulled on me. I was so close to her, our noses were touching.

"Pinky swear, my ass. You better not say a word," she said, fire in her eyes.

I zipped my lips and threw away the imaginary key. Cashmere laughed and took a seat on the chair at her desk. She sat backward so she could face me. I settled in on her bed again, this time, grabbing her pillows and getting comfortable.

"I was sitting in the living room one day, reading."

"Wait. How long ago was this?" I butted in.

She gave me a look. "I thought I was the one who asked a lot of questions."

I giggled. "Okay. Okay. Sorry."

"Mama and Emé must've come in through the garage because I didn't even hear them until I *heard* them" she continued, putting quotation marks in the air. "Anyway, I was reading my summer reading for English. I remember the time because it was right before we went back to school."

I couldn't believe Cashmere had been able to hold water about something for almost nine months. School would be over in a little over a month. I chuckled on the inside.

"I guess the conversation started in the car, long before they even pulled into the garage, but it wasn't so bad. I heard Emé say it was different for her because no matter how Mama made her feel, she would never be *her* child."

I nodded. I always knew Emé had issues with that. "She's told us that before."

"Yeah," Cashmere continued, "but the way she sounded was different. It wasn't like the "Thank you, Mama for always being there for me and accepting me as your own," voice she usually would use. It was more like "I don't need your pity because I had a mother before you" kind of voice."

"So, pain?"

Cashmere shrugged. "Yeah, pain, I guess you could say that. Anyway, I heard them shuffling around in the kitchen, so I got up to go see what they'd bought. Just thinking I'd join in on the girl chat and they would move onto another topic."

Cashmere's phone went off again. I grunted.

"Relax, baby sis," she said, hitting ignore again. "Your time is coming"

She winked at me, and I stuck my tongue out at her.

"Go on. What happened?" I said.

"I'd never seen Mama look like this before. We've had some crazy family issues, but nothing where she had that look on her face like she'd lost someone."

I was quiet now.

Cashmere leaned forward and dropped her voice down. "Emé was still going on about something, but I couldn't make out everything. As soon as I hit the door and was about to go in to calm them down, Emé blurted out that it was Mama's fault she'd even gotten rid of it. That if it hadn't been for her prodding and encouraging it, she wouldn't have ever gotten rid of the baby."

I swallowed the lump that was lodged in my throat. As soon as Cashmere said it, I felt the pressure rising in my gut. I wasn't sure if it was the wooziness I'd been feeling the last few days or the fact that Emé's secret was a massive blow.

"She had an abortion? Are you sure that's what she said?"

Cashmere cut her eyes at me. "See, this is why I didn't want to tell you. Emé can do no wrong in your mind. But honestly, I wouldn't have believed it either if I hadn't heard it with my own ears."

I ignored her smart comment. I didn't think Emé could do no wrong. I just didn't think she would ever do me wrong. I thought that of all my siblings because we always protected each other. Cashmere included.

"From everything I pieced together, Emé was fourteen when she got pregnant. She was messing around with some senior at school and he knocked her up. I don't even think Mama and Papa involved his parents. They just got it done."

I rested my chin in my hands. "They probably didn't even let her tell him."

Cashmere snapped her fingers. "You know what? You're probably right. So, anyway, Emé goes on and on about how she would've kept her baby, but Mama said it wasn't fair for Emé to blame her because she was the one that cried she wouldn't be able to pursue her dreams if she had a baby. Not to mention, Emé said she didn't even like the guy."

Cashmere paused when her phone chimed. She grabbed it and sent out a text. "He's a pain in the ass," she huffed. "Anyway, this is when Mama pulled her power move. When it all came tumbling down for Emé."

I smiled. Mama had a way of saying things that made it clear that you needed to fall in line. Period. You could be mad, kick, scream and shout, but it was a done deal. Papa often found himself on the other side of those moments as well.

"She said, and I quote: 'Emé, you're the one who walks around here carrying a monkey on your back about a decision you made. Your father signed the papers because you kicked and screamed about how it would stop your life and how you didn't want to be somebody's deadbeat baby mama. Don't put your demons on me because I was able to have another baby in my thirties. You need to get yourself together before either of us says something we'll regret.' And that was it. Emé was silent."

I knew how she felt. I don't even think Cashmere realized the bomb she just dropped or the secret tied to it. *Don't put your demons on me because I was able to have another baby in my thirties.* I replayed that line in my head over and over again. I could even hear Mama's voice saying it. Is that the reason Emé and I were so close? Was it because I was the child she never had? Is that why Mama was so protective? Because she felt Emé was trying to overpower her decisions when it came to me?

Now that I recall, there wasn't a time that I asked Emé for something or to do something, and she said no.

"Isn't that crazy?" Cashmere asked, breaking me out of my thoughts.

I nodded. "What's even crazier," I said, shifting myself so that I was sitting straight up, "is that we wouldn't have ever known if you didn't hear their argument. I don't get the big deal. Mama's told us some deep stuff. So has Papa. We all have stuff."

I was trying to make sense of it being such a big secret that a teenage girl had an abortion to secure her future. I know we didn't necessarily believe in them as a Christian family, but my parents were realistic. They prayed and did what they felt was best. In this case, it seems they did what Emé wanted.

"See, Brelyn, this is what I mean –"

I raised my hand to stop her. "Don't say it again. I'm so sick of you telling me that I have on rose colored glasses when I don't. I know more than you think I do. If I didn't, I wouldn't have known that you had an abortion last year."

I hadn't meant to say it, and I honestly wasn't even sure if it was true, but a part of me had a feeling that Cashmere was hiding and doing a lot of stuff that she had no business doing at sixteen. She spaced out for a few minutes, confirming that what I thought I knew was indeed true. I'd heard the crying at night. I'd seen the stiff walking for the seven days. And I remembered the two months she didn't get her period. As sisters, ours worked like clockwork. I knew.

"Don't judge me," she said, nostrils flaring. "I did what I had to."

I stood up and grabbed her in a hug. "That's my point, Cash. I'm not judging you. So don't judge, Emé." I grabbed her face and looked dead into her eyes. "I love you, sis. And for the record, I never told anyone about that."

She closed her eyes, and the tears fell. She laughed, causing some snot to come out her nose. "You make me sick."

I knew she was teasing. I walked back over to the bed, grabbing her hand and bringing her with me.

"You know too much," she said, wiping her face. "You're too smart for your own good. Saith better be careful."

I laughed. "Whatever. Stop acting like lupus equals dummy. It doesn't."

She looked at me and grabbed my hands. "I don't say those things because of your sickness. I say them because you're the baby. I honestly don't want you to grow up." She sighed and looked back at her phone. "The sooner you do the sooner you find out just how cold this world really is."

Chapter 12

I rushed into school, waving at Papa quickly before he pulled off. I pushed past the ache in my knee and made it to my locker without running into anyone. Taking out the books I needed, I headed to my first-period business class. I was glad it was my Entrepreneurship class because I'd get to show everyone what I'd been working on for Bodies by Brelyn. The only thing that made me hesitant was the fact that I had to talk about my lupus. I wasn't sure what I was so afraid of. My father's *Forbes.com* cover story a few months ago had pretty much shed a huge light on my disease.

When they'd asked him if they could do the story, it was centered around the theme, 'A Father's Family,' showing that every self-made billionaire had a family behind him that kept him grounded. My father almost gave up hope after his own battle with cancer, but when I was diagnosed, he'd stopped going to church and praying for a whole month. Forbes was able to capture the essence of his business and how he balances it so well with family. My diagnosis pushed him to find the balance he needed.

Since I attended school a few days a week at any given time, I had to stay on top of everything at home. I barely had time for friends outside of my siblings. Being a Clover had its moments, and I never got too comfortable. As I settled into my seat, I waved at Rebecca. She was cool, and I could hang with her every now and then. We'd just started getting closer after working on an English project together. She stood up and walked over to my desk.

"Hey, Brelyn," she said. "What's new with you?"

"Same stuff, different day," I said. "How's class been going?"

Catching up with class online was cool, but being filled in on the things face to face was much better. It was like watching a favorite episode that you missed on Hulu, and I knew that Rebecca would tell me everything important that I missed.

"You know Kara got kicked out for plagiarizing her business project? She presented it while you were away and when Mrs. Barber noticed it had similarities to something she'd seen before, she investigated and found out it was the project of a former student from two years ago. I mean, Kara, you couldn't have found something that was like twelve years old?" Rebecca rambled on.

Rebecca was cute, a little curvy and very bubbly. The whole time she was telling me this story, she scrolled through her cell phone, probably liking every picture of Coy Abraham, a junior she had a major crush on.

"That's a bit extreme for plagiarizing one project," I said, situating myself so I could get ready to present. I opened up my MacBook and pulled up the stuff I needed. "She must've done something else."

"Sucked Lance off during second-period gym," she whispered, then put a finger to her lips.

I looked at her with my mouth hanging open, and she nodded. All I could do was shake my head and laugh. The Philadelphia Business and Arts Academy was a school that sat in the top six magnet schools in Philadelphia. A school driven by tuition and scholarships, most dad's sent their daughters here thinking they would be safe from the public school system's worries and woes, only to discover that most of those things happened twice as much in a private school than they did in public. Private school junkies felt like they had something to prove while public school kids felt they were the real deal. My school hadn't been around when Emé was in high school, but the three of us knew of stories that could put Monica Lewinsky's to shame.

"Well, you feeling any better?" Rebecca continued.

I pursed my lips. It was hard explaining to people how I was feeling. I mean, there's no words for it and some days, I may not feel anything at all. What I did know is that I was still learning exactly what lupus is and how it affects the body.

"You'll see," was all I said as our teacher walked in.

Ms. Barber smiled and winked at me. She mouthed 'good to have you back,' and I waved. I liked her a lot. Her and her husband, who together owned a small hotel in Florida, had been over to our house several times when my father had his business functions.

"Okay, class," she said, placing her messenger bag on her desk. A few stragglers came in and took their seats. They were met with icy eyes and a warning finger. Everyone knew Ms. Barber would call your parents *after* she'd given you a piece of her mind for not following directions. She expected us in our seats two minutes before class started or you were late.

"I'm so excited for our next presentation. With the end of the year rapidly approaching," she turned to the calendar and quickly counted the days, "we have about four weeks left, so we're going to take the rest of this week and all of the next to hear some presentations. Then, we'll get started on what you'll need for the final."

Groans and moans fluttered throughout the classroom. Rebecca raised her hand.

"I thought you said the presentations were our final," she said, without waiting for Ms. Barber to call on her.

"I lied," she said, crossing her arms. "I changed my mind, but this final won't be a standard final. I promise, it'll be fun, and you'll learn a lot." She waited for the class to quiet down. "I'm excited to introduce Brelyn's project, Bodies by Brelyn, which I know some of you are familiar with because you've been to one of her leg burning aerobics classes."

Some of the students clapped, Rebecca patted my arm and gave me a thumbs up, and Kevin Carson shouted.

"Kevin," Ms. Barber scolded. "Calm down; your whole team can hear you."

Everyone laughed. Kevin came to a few of my classes when he injured his ankle playing soccer. He was a huge supporter from day one. Turning my attention back to Ms. Barber, I noticed she had already pulled my website up on the projector.

"Brelyn had to make some changes due to her illness, which I believe God will heal in His timing. What she came up with is just as brilliant as what she had before, but she chose a different business model. Whenever you're ready, Brelyn," she said, waving me up.

Just as I stood up, I saw my phone light up. Mrs. Barber was looking at her own cell phone, so I bent down to see who it was. It was a text from Saith. *Looking forward to hanging after school. See you later, Bre.* ☺

I'd gotten used to the butterflies in my stomach, surprising myself anytime I didn't smile when he sent me a text message. We'd talked over the last couple of days, but everything was short and quick. His father was out of town on business, and he was keeping an eye on Myla who was making me feel comfortable one minute and not so much the next.

Most of the time, I told Saith that I would talk to him later because she was always looming over his shoulder. I threw my phone back in my bag and walked to the front. I inserted the flash drive just as I heard gum cracking coming from the back of the class.

"Rebecca. Trash it," Mrs. Barber said without even looking up from her phone. "That was my hubby. Sorry everyone."

"Yes. No phones, Mrs. Barber," Kevin teased.

She was the one who had come up with the rule. She rolled her eyes at Kevin playfully and put her phone in her purse. "Yes, sir."

We all laughed. This is why everyone loved Mrs. Barber. She gave down to earth a whole new meaning. When my website filled the screen, I cleared my throat and started my presentation.

"Okay. Hey guys, good to be back," I started. "Bodies By Brelyn was in need of a makeover, and I decided to go in the direction that would benefit not just myself, but others who will have difficulty attending regular classes."

I looked up. Everyone's eyes were fixed on the projector. I continued.

"I chose to do a subscription based business model, basically offering a nutrition plan, a fitness plan or a consulting plan depending on the needs of my client. When you subscribe to the website for forty dollars a month, you get a ten-minute workout each month, coupons for food shopping and a 'get started' meal plan. I just added this to the website after being contacted by someone through Twitter. She needed a quick plan, but she's only seventeen and is limited by her budget."

I scrolled down to show the package I'd created for Paris. "For eighty dollars, I sent her a breakfast meal plan for the week and a morning workout that she could do to get started. That's when it hit me that if people could subscribe to the site and get free stuff monthly at a low price point, they would be more likely to take advantage of other services, such as the Full Body Workout Kit or the Leg Kit."

I used the laser to direct the class' attention to the top of the site where my menu sat. "Here is where you get to see the different kits." I clicked on the Kits Tab. "Each kit comes with customized workouts for various conditions. If you're struggling with obesity or childhood diabetes, or lupus," I said, "then you would go to the Ease Into It Kit option. If you're an athlete such as our beloved Kevin here, you can choose the Get With It Kit."

"That's a cool name for a tough guy like myself," Kevin said. The class laughed.

"I noticed you changed the color layout Brelyn," Mrs. Barber said. "Why is that?"

"I wanted it to be unisex. Yellow works for that."

Ms. Barber nodded. I continued on for the next ten minutes, then took questions for ten more.

"Where can I sign up?" Taylor asked. "I've been trying to get into working out again."

Everyone, including Mrs. Barber, looked at Taylor. I wasn't sure what she was trying to do, but her 100-pound frame didn't need much working out. Either way, I would never turn down a client. I scrolled over another tab.

"You can sign up here. You'll get a message back within twenty-four hours, and we'll discuss packages from there."

I looked around. "If there are no more questions, that's it."

A round of applause rang out across the room. I took a bow and grabbed my flash drive before taking my seat. The last fifteen minutes of class consisted of Mrs. Barber saying who would present next week and giving us a massive reading assignment that would help with our final. I looked at the clock and groaned. I had at least four more hours before I'd get to see Saith Richards.

❋ ❋ ❋

He was waiting for me at the front doors of the school at dismissal.

"Hey, pretty girl," he said. "How was your presentation?"

He grabbed my bag and put it on his lap. I got behind him and pushed his wheelchair as I told him about the presentation.

"I go to the doctor's Friday," he said.

"Check-up?"

He nodded. "The paralysis was always temporary, so they want to do a couple of tests to see if my limbs and body react to everything like it should at this stage."

"That's good news, right?" I touched his shoulder.

"Yeah. If it works," Saith said. I could hear the pain in his voice.

"You can always find a summer league to play for," I continued. "And let's not forget, you could train children or work at a school over the summer."

"Don't worry about it," he said, changing the subject. "Did anyone sign up after you were done?"

"Ms. Barber told them to do it from their phones or laptops. I got two emails. I'll see when I read them later."

He smiled. "What kind of business school has a policy where you can't sell your business on site?"

"Yeah, they implemented it last year after some students took advantage of the whole selling policy. I guess illegal drugs wasn't part of the plan."

Saith looked up at me. "You're kidding?"

"Nope. At the end of the day, we're all rich kids who live in a world that tells us we're still missing out on something."

"That's true. I was looking at my Instagram last night. This kid I know from Chicago was doing so well. Had the scholarship, the girls, strong family background, everything. He got locked up two weeks ago for murder. Sadly, he really did do it. I thought it was some kind of setup, but he turned himself in."

I listened intently. It was the very thing my parents feared. Us getting caught up and making one mistake that could cost us our lives. For some people, it was the norm to live in an environment where things like that just happened and life continued on as usual. My parents had grown up in it. As much as I loved visiting North Philadelphia, the truth was, there wasn't much good left when it came to schools, recreation centers and other services that helped keep kids off the streets. Either the city closed it down, or the city officials found ways to pour more money into other things.

"Hey, you still with me?" Saith asked. "You not bugged out because I mentioned girls, are you?"

I stopped pushing and walked alongside him. "No. Not at all. I was thinking about what you said, and then it hit me."

He raised an eyebrow at me. "What?"

"You lost your scholarship? Didn't you?"

He looked ahead and kept pushing without saying anything. He'd been rambling on about the kid in Chicago, and I'd noticed how he swallowed when he said 'scholarship.'

"They said there's no way I would get into position to play by the start of next school year. It's conditional, but..."

"But what? What's the condition?" I took my ringing phone out of my bag. "Give me one second. Hey, Mom. Yes, Saith and I are walking together. No. Well, did you call her phone? I didn't see Cashmere, and Desmond is with his club. Okay. Yes. I'll see you in fifteen minutes. Love you more."

I hung up and sighed. "Moms," I said to Saith, putting my phone in my back pocket. I moved my hair out of my face and looked at him again. I realized what I'd said.

"I'm sorry."

He looked at me and faked a smile. "Stop. Don't do that. Are you not supposed to talk about your mom because mine isn't here? That's dumb."

I smiled weakly. "So...what's the condition?"

I'd had to fight to get Mama to let me walk home, but the twenty-minute walk gave us time to talk.

"I have to be able to do a one-mile run, a thirty-second sprint and a whole bunch of upper body and lower body exercises that ain't happenin'," he continued.

"By when?"

"Neverwery. It's not happening, Bre."

I sighed in frustration. "Would you stop giving up so easy? What if I would've done that with my business? You know, I find that so amazing. You can push me to do and be the best, but you can't find it for yourself. I thought basketball was everything to you."

I knew I was hitting him hard, but he needed it. I was over his nonchalant attitude. I'd seen it too many times in the courtyard; I'd seen it with Myla and his father, and now he was doing it with me.

"You gonna do arm lifts in my yard forever?"

I knew I'd gone too far. But it was too late.

"Nope," he said. "I'm not. No worries. I won't burden you anymore." He pushed faster toward home. I ran a little to catch up with him, grabbing the handles of his chair roughly. The pain that shot up my arm was fierce. I didn't even have time to react.

"Bre, let's not have this discussion," he said, still moving. I was bent over holding my arm. I guess it took him a minute to realize I wasn't with him. He stopped, turned around and came rushing back in my direction. By the time he got back to me, he was breathing in overtime.

"Bre, what's wrong? You want me to call your mom?" he asked, grabbing my bag and reaching for my phone. I grabbed it back.

"No, I just grabbed your handles too quick," I sputtered. "I'm fine."

"You're not fine," he said, lightly touching my arm. "Does that hurt?"

I shook my head. "No. It hurts up here," I said, rubbing my shoulder.

He pulled me onto his lap, making my book bag drop on the ground, and started rubbing my shoulder gently. "Maybe if you do that arm thing you taught me, it'll help until we get you home."

I winced. I had taken a few deep breaths before I realized what had happened. He'd pulled me on his lap with the same ease of the night he lifted me in the courtyard. After rubbing my shoulder for a few minutes, I slowly stood up. Saith grabbed my waist gently and turned my face to his. I had never kissed anyone romantically before, but when his lips hit mine, I knew that it was supposed to feel like this. Suddenly, the pain in my shoulder was long forgotten.

Chapter 13

When we got home, Saith went straight to his house, and I went to mine. After the kiss, we just parted ways and continued on like nothing happened. My arm was still a little sore, but I was hoping Papa was home by now. He was the cushion between Mama and me when we knocked heads.

"Papa," I said, relieved to see him reading in the living room.

He put his book down and opened his arms. "Hey, baby girl. How was school?"

He gripped me tight and kissed my cheek. Even if I'd wanted to hide it, his grip made me squeal. He pushed up off the couch, pulling me up with him.

"What's going on?" he asked.

"I think I pulled a muscle."

"How? What did you do after school?"

"Nothing. I was just walking home with Saith..."

"The neighbor?" he asked, his face contorted.

"Yes. I think it's just a little strained."

"How would you have pulled an arm muscle just walking home? Is it your lupus, Bre?" he sighed. "You can't be afraid to tell us if something is wrong. Every pain issue doesn't mean a trip to the hospital."

Tears stung my eyes. "I know. I know. I've been feeling some pain in my knee, but I didn't want to scare myself."

He picked up the phone. "I'm calling Dr. Warhol now." He sighed and placed the phone to his ear while he continued talking to me. "The whole purpose of having a room set up here is so you don't have to be scared of the hospital. It makes no sense that you wouldn't say anything, Brelyn. None."

He was still rubbing my shoulder while talking to Dr. Warhol, but I could feel the tension in his body as I leaned against him. I cried into his belly just as Cashmere came walking through the door. We both looked at her.

"Okay, Doctor. See you when you get here," my father said, ending his call. "And where were you?" he said, turning to Cashmere. "You should've walked home with your sister. Was that Robbie that dropped you off?"

Cashmere's eyes grew wide, and she slowly walked into the living room. "No. It was Courtney."

I wondered at that moment which Courtney it was. The boy Courtney who she'd been with on a break from Robbie or her girlfriend Courtney who she hadn't spoken to in two years. Papa kept his eyes locked on her while trying to comfort me.

"You okay, Brelyn? Why are you crying?" Cashmere asked, reverting my father's attention back to me. She walked over and grabbed my hand. "Daddy, you need my help with anything? I heard you talking to the doctor."

My dad's expression softened. "No. He should be here shortly. I'll go get your mother. She's napping."

He turned and headed upstairs, and I glared at my sister. "How's Courtney?" I asked.

She scowled at me. "Better than Robbie," she whispered. "I'll get you some water, Bre," she said, loudly.

She put her fingers to her lips and headed to the kitchen. I leaned back against the sofa and closed my eyes. I'd kissed Saith and had an attack all in one day. If things could just keep looking up from here, life would be good.

🌸🌸🌸

Dr. Warhol stood over me, administering medicine through the IV stuck in my arm. I looked around the room taking in everything that reminded me of the very place I didn't want to be – the bag hanging over my shoulder with the line running through to my arm, the reclining bed, the hospital gown I wore and the smell of Dr. Warhols' gloves every time he was within an inch of my face – all rang hospital. I hadn't been in this room since Papa first set it up a few months ago. I looked over at Mama as he grabbed my left arm and started to massage it gently.

"Just relax," he said. "Let me know if you feel any pain."

I nodded while still looking at Mama. She was holding a tissue in her hand, dabbing at the corner of her eyes. Papa was standing up behind her, watching Dr. Warhol like a hawk. I didn't even need to look to my other side to see if Cashmere or Desmond were there. I could hear Cashmere texting on her phone, and I could hear Desmond's music through his earphones. They were trying to make this feel as normal as possible.

"So, will I still be able to work on my computer and stuff?" I asked the doctor.

My father cleared his throat. "Not a priority right now," he said, giving Mama's shoulder a reassuring squeeze. "Stay focused, Bre."

When Dr. Warhol walked to my other side, I took a look at Desmond. He winked at me and gave me a thumbs up. "Don't worry," he mouthed.

I wasn't sure what freaked me out more. The fact that everyone said not to worry when there was a needle sticking out of my arm in my home or the idea that Papa was having second thoughts about even letting me run an online business. He told Mama that Saith and I walked home together and that was when I'd felt the pain. She came downstairs right before Dr. Warhol arrived and scolded me.

"You have a friend that would allow you to even push his wheelchair? Does that make any kind of sense to you, Brelyn?" she had said. "I'm going to call his father. I think you two need a break."

"I already asked him to come over later tonight," Papa continued. "We'll talk to him."

Of course I protested, but once Dr. Warhol read off the facts, telling my parents what was wrong and what I needed to do to get better, I had no choice but to nod in agreement.

"Can I at least still take online clients?" I asked. "Just maybe two a week?"

Mama gave me a death stare. "I'm not going to entertain this right now. And neither are you." She sighed and stood up. "Are you even listening to the doctor? Repeat back to me what he just told you."

She crossed her arms and waited for my response. "That I need to rest, stay hydrated, stick to my nutritionist's orders and stop stressing. But, my business doesn't stress me," I added, finishing up. "It's not like I physically work out with my clients. Being a trainer is different."

Mama squinted, but Papa stepped in before she could say anything. He looked at her, giving her a slight nod. She sat down.

"Bre, listen to me," he said. "I love you and so does everyone in here. Saith is just some boy who likes you."

I sat up slowly. "What does my business have to do with Saith? I'm talking about Bodies by Brelyn. I know this afternoon was a bit much, but it was all innocent fun. We were just walking home from school."

I was pleading my case. Cashmere looked up from her phone and gave me a weak smile.

"I'm sure she was just fooling around," she said to my parents. "There's no reason to take away what makes her happy because of that, is it?"

I looked at her with tears in my eyes. A few minutes ago, I was on the verge of tears because of the pain in my body. Now, it was because of the pain in my heart. *Being a Clover is about more than having the name. It's about the legacy.* My father's words kept ringing in my ears. I wanted nothing more than to keep at it. Even *Cool Cash* was getting raves on Instagram. Desmond's *Bricks* just pulled in an offer from a major company. Emé didn't even need her skin care line and half the time I wasn't even sure she wanted it since she was killing the theater scene. Did I have to come in fourth just because I was the fourth child?

"Papa," I whined, "you said that being online was better. So, what's the problem?"

"So you mean you weren't sneaking out at night training Saith? To help him get back on the court, right?"

I sat there silent. I'd heard him say it, I just wasn't sure how he'd found out. Then it hit me. Saith's father must've told him. That's why Papa invited him over for dinner tonight. It probably hadn't been intentional, but my anger level went up a notch. It seemed like everyone around me was involved in decisions about me, including the neighbors. Mr. Richards couldn't even keep his own family in order, and he'd somehow managed to insert himself into mine.

"It was just a few times –"

My father raised his hand, hushing me immediately. "I don't give a damn if it was a half of one time. You think we do these things to punish you? It's for your own good."

Desmond pulled out his earphones. He looked at Papa.

"Dad, I'm sure Bre was just trying to help," he said softly. "Don't punish her for doing what you raised us to do."

Papa turned to Desmond. "And exactly what is that?"

"Help people," he said. "It may have been misguided, and she should've stopped when she felt her body telling her to, but I talked to Saith and Brelyn. Nobody's trying to do anything crazy here."

Desmond had Papa's full attention. "And by anything crazy you mean, nobody is trying to have sex with my daughter and get killed?"

Desmond smirked. I looked at Mama. She was silently watching. When Papa did the disciplining, Mama stepped back. When Mama did it, Papa stepped back, but they were always on the same page, neither one of them undermining each other. It was like they had spider senses to silently communicate.

"Daddy," I squealed. "I'm not having sex."

I cut my eyes at Cashmere. I swear that girl had put a target on my back with her ruthless actions. She frowned at me and gave me a 'what the hell' look.

"I never said that you were," Papa said.

Dr. Warhol cleared his throat and excused himself. "I'll come back in thirty minutes to check her vitals."

His demeanor changed when we mentioned sex. He left without another word. Papa didn't continue until he heard the door slam.

"Bre, this isn't just about Saith. You've been disregarding things that matter to your health since you were diagnosed. We all noticed it."

I looked at everyone in the room. It was funny how all at once, they looked at each other or down at their laps. I crossed my arms.

"Is that what everyone thinks? That I don't care?"

Desmond stood up and walked over to the bed. "Bre, you act like we're just here to help keep you in check. When are you going to start taking this more serious? I don't want to lose my baby sister," he said.

Cashmere came and stood on my other side, squeezing my hand. "Exactly. Listen," she said, putting her phone in her pocket. I noticed it light up just as she did that. "I know our parents can be a bit smothering, but we all agree that you need to take a few steps back and relax. It seems like we're the ones reminding you about the food you need to eat, the medicine you need to take. Do you even keep your schedule in your phone like you used to?'

My eyes shot back and forth between her and Desmond. I was ready to be on the defense, but I realized that they were right. I had been so caught up in trying not to be sick that I ignored the fact that I was. I was the one causing myself not to enjoy life just because I assumed I couldn't have the life I wanted with lupus.

"I wasn't doing it on purpose," I said, defeated. "I'm scared, and it's not fair."

My parents came and stood on each side of me. Desmond and Cash sat on the edge of my bed, moving out the way for our parents. No one said anything about the missing spot that belonged to Emé. She would've been right here, rubbing some part of my body to let me know everything was okay. Mama looked at where I was staring.

"She's in Boston, said she'd call later."

I looked at Mama blankly. She could feed that excuse to someone else. I wasn't falling for it because I knew that Emé would've told me that herself. For now, I would go along with it.

"No worries," I said. "I didn't mean to scare you guys. I just feel like everyone is pitying me. Your actions are just another reminder that I'm sick."

Mama grabbed my hand. "Because you are. Even with believing in God's healing power, we don't ignore the facts. We just pray for healing, knowing that things can change."

I smiled and wiped my eyes. "I know. I know. I just wish things were different."

"We all do," Cashmere said. "We all do."

She grabbed one of the tissues from Mama and wiped at her eyes. Desmond sniffled playfully.

"All these girls, Pop," he said, grabbing Papa's shoulder, "what are we gonna do?"

Papa forced a smile. "Honestly, this is one of those moments where I'm not even sure."

Everyone stopped smiling, and we all looked at Papa. A tear dropped from his eye. Desmond walked around to his side and turned him to face him. Mama rubbed his back.

"We're Clovers. Crying doesn't mean dying."

Papa hugged Desmond tight. They stayed like that for a minute before everyone started turning their attention back to me. Cashmere's face was super wet, and so was Mama's. I giggled.

"All these snotty noses," I said. "Shouldn't I be the one crying?"

Everyone laughed and crowded back around my bed. "I promise from this day forward to take things more serious. I won't give up, and I'll take the time to learn more about lupus. Papa, I have to work on the website for school. It's a part of my business class."

"Desmond told me that already, but no clients. Period. Even though you aren't physically working out yourself, running a business is stressful. People are stressful. You need to relax."

It was a demand. I could hear it in his voice.

"What about Saith? Are you saying we can't be friends?"

I knew neither Mama nor Papa would say who I could be friends with. They didn't operate that way with any of us. But Saith was different. I knew it, and so did they.

"Bre, he's sixteen. I know that's not that big of a deal, but with all that's going on, I have my concerns."

"Ditto," Mama said. "But, I know that you see something in him that we haven't gotten to know yet. So, we're going old school with it."

Cashmere grunted. "You are not about to do that to her, are you?"

Mama pinched her arm.

"Ouch!"

"Keep playing, and we'll do it to you too. We'll have our talk later," she scolded, giving Cashmere a look.

"What's old school?" I said, looking at Desmond.

"We'll be sitting right there with you and Saith while you guys hang out," Papa said, putting his arm around Mama's neck. He pulled her close to him and kissed her temple. "Right there," Papa emphasized this with his finger. "Sitting right between you two."

"Well, that won't be hard, considering," Cashmere teased.

I knew pushing back would make it worse, so I gave in. "Nothing is going on. I offered to train him, so don't blame Saith and treat him bad."

"We don't blame him," Mama said. "He was an innocent bystander."

Everyone laughed while I sat there trying to figure out a way to keep things going without allowing my parents to bust my groove.

🍀🍀🍀

Later that night I woke up sweating. I didn't realize where I was until I heard the dripping of the IV. I took a few deep breaths and sat up. The digital clock on the nightstand read four AM. I threw my legs over the bed and waited a few seconds before standing up. The dizziness crept over me quickly. I leaned against the bed and caught my balance. Grabbing the IV cart, I headed to the bathroom. Other than feeling woozy, the pain was gone. I could tell whatever Dr. Warhol had done worked instantly.

Other than the typical restrictions, he encouraged me to lead a full, active life. I was glad when he told my parents that living with the fear of getting hurt was worse than actually getting hurt. I was a healthy teen, considering my condition. I had to live my life. After I was done, I stood up and looked at myself in the mirror. My hair was brushed back in a bun, courtesy of Mama. She even gave me a facial with one of Emé's products.

I walked back to my bed, poured myself a cup of water and reached for my phone. My laptop was nowhere in sight. I

122

figured my parents would take it away so I wouldn't be tempted to do any work. I opened my email app and saw six new messages. Two were from Emé.

The first one was short and sweet.

Baby sis,

Sorry for my absence lately. I'm in Boston and will be home in two days. I called you a few times to check on you. Mama told me you were sick and that Dr. Warhol would be there to take care of you. He's one of the best. Love you. E

The second one was more in-depth and had a few surprises.

Hey, baby sis. I know you're probably cursing me out under your breath since I know you would never curse in front of the King and Queen, but I had a trip to Boston planned with Derrick before you got sick. I'm sorry we haven't talked much lately, but I've been going through some of my own stuff. I never told you how I feel about my mother's death and I never thought anything of it since we're all a big happy family. But nothing will ever come in between our bond. Please don't tell Mama about this email, but I promise when I get back to Philly, we'll hang out, and I'll talk to you about my mother. Maybe you can be my therapist for a change? Love you more than you know. E.

Besides the fact that she'd mentioned her mother, I could read the sarcasm dripping from her comment about being "a big happy family." It was as if she was taking a shot at Mama and Papa. As much as I loved and adored my siblings, my parents were my heroes. I always felt like I was being pulled in so many different directions when it came to the Clover clan. As if being all in with one meant going against the others. I knew that wasn't true, but my mind was boggled with a number of times I'd been the peacemaker, the balance between a heated moment and a damn near blow over. I often felt like the cushion that everybody felt safe to come lean on.

I scrolled through rest of the emails and dabbed at my eyes. Thinking about my family in this way always brought me to tears. My eyes landed on two emails from Paris Rivers.

I opened the first one, which had been sent around six yesterday evening. Dr. Warhol had arrived at four thirty. I didn't know what I was going to tell her, but I couldn't just ignore her. She'd already paid, and we'd already started. Not to mention, she purchased another kit a few days ago, adding a weekly meal plan.

Hi Brelyn,

I hope all is well. I've been sticking to my breakfast meal plan and wanted to discuss the weekly plan you sent me. I'm actually coming to Philly to visit family after school is over. I'll be done May 25th. It's different here in the South. I know up there, you guys get out later, but I'd love to link up when I come to town. I'll probably purchase a consulting package sometime soon. PS The new job is going well. I think I'll be closer to my weight loss goals sooner than I expected.

Talk to you soon, Paris

From what I'd learned, Paris and her family lived in Atlanta. I thought her name was interesting. I hit reply and wrote back:

Hey Paris,

Thanks so much for reaching out. I'm going to touch base with you about your weekly nutrition plan by tomorrow. I will also let you know how my schedule looks for anything after May 30th. Thanks again for trying out Bodies by Brelyn.

Best,

Brelyn M. Clover

I kept it short and sweet. No promises made, no promises need to be kept. I scrolled back to Emé's message and hit reply.

Hey Big E,

I can't wait to see you. It's been too long since we had a good day together. Let's hang out. Leave Derrick at home this time (just kidding). I have so much to tell you. Love you always,

Bre

I couldn't wait to see my sis and have a girl talk. I was just hoping that when we did talk, I could forget all about the secret I should've never been told.

Chapter 14

Two weeks later Emé and I sat across from each other on our first day out together in what seemed like forever.

"You always look beautiful, E," I said, biting into my spinach salad. I'd already eaten the grilled chicken that was on top. Had Emé not insisted on the balsamic vinaigrette, I would've asked the lady to douse my salad in ranch dressing. I was all for eating healthy and sticking to my diet, but every once in awhile, eating what I wanted would be nice. I decided not to resist. At least I was out of the house.

Emé returned a week after our email exchange, but I still had to wait another week before we got to sit down and have a private moment. She'd made it to the house for the Mother's Day dinner Desmond always cooked for mom and in time to see him off to his prom.

"Thanks, Bre," she said. "I just know the ten pounds I've gained is due to all this stress. I can't stand it."

I opened my sparkling water and chugged it down. "Yuck. I swear tap water is better."

She laughed. "You can't drink that stuff. It's not good and not good for *you*."

"What are you stressing about? Is it the Spa or Hollywood?"

She finished her water and held her hand up to get the waiter's attention. "Can you bring us a pitcher of your Evian spring water with lemons and limes on the side?"

"My pleasure, ma'am," he said, removing some of the dishes off of the table.

"Bre, you've known me long enough to know that what comes easily to me isn't hardly something that can stress me. Even on my worst days, I still feel like I'm walking on a cloud."

"Is it Noni? I know having a business partner can be stressful."

"She's fine. I thought it would be hard at first, working with a best friend, but she's the dermatologist, and I'm the esthetician. My focus is the skincare side; it makes it easier."

"I have no idea how you pulled it off, but two bull-headed women running any kind of business together is interesting. I pray your staff is prepared to intervene when you guys try to kill each other."

She balled up her fist and punched the air in my direction. "Don't make me hurt you."

After the waiter had dropped off our water, I sat back and stared at my sister. Emé had everything going for herself. She started her skincare line three years ago, after she'd traveled with a few stage plays and finished two films in New York. She managed to work her way into the hearts of America and into their homes with a recurring role on a television show. In addition, she was a licensed esthetician. When Dad gave her the seed money, she sat down with a colleague with a chemistry degree, and they went through everything, testing samples and making sure the line would be great for ethnic women; and her skincare line was born.

I understood why she was stressed out at a time like this. The Boston trip was for her final performance in a play that was doing extremely well across the nation. She was auditioning and connecting with her agent, but she wasn't sure what was lined up after the play. Emé's life had to be mapped out, controlled and in order. If it wasn't and you didn't know her, Emé's wrath could shake you up. But with us, it was just that – a wrath much like Papa's. You just had to lay low until it blew over.

"How come you never talk about your mom?" I didn't mean to be so blunt about it, but at least I opened the door for her to address it. I knew that it was bothering her.

"Bre, it's not an easy subject," she said. "I figure it's easier to just move on and deal with her death in my own way. Dad's moved on. Why can't I?"

I felt a chill go up my spine. I frowned. Certainly, she knew that Dad would move on. Right?

"I'm just kidding," she said, patting my hand. "The truth is, I always have a hard time around this time of year because it's when she passed away. I get too involved in my feelings and I act like the world is supposed to stop."

She had tears in her eyes, so I thought a joke would help. "You think like that every day."

She winked. "Yeah, yeah. But honestly, it's not something you or anyone else can help me with. I just have to pray and let it go."

My mouth was starting to feel dry. I drank some more water. "But that's what I don't get. Why do you have to let your mother go? We're your family. We're here to help you. Mom loves you like you're her own. Isn't that enough?"

Her eyes grew wide, and her nostrils flared. "Sherese Clover will never be enough to replace Rita Shepard." She huffed and sat back in the chair.

I threw my hands up, biting my bottom lip. "That came out wrong. I wasn't saying that nor was I insinuating that she could replace your mother. I was just saying, Mom's love and our love is enough to help you get through it." I reached out and grabbed her hand. "Emé. We love you. You know that."

She didn't say anything. Her eyes filled with tears, but she wouldn't let them fall.

"Tell me about your mom. Rita? Doesn't that mean 'pearl' in Spanish?"

Emé started smiling. "Leave it to my smart baby sister to know that off the top of her head."

I wanted to tell her how I knew, but I didn't want to break the rhythm of our conversation. I'd been eavesdropping on a conversation she had with my father when I was little. That's the only time I remember her mother being talked about in depth.

"Was it hard growing up being half black and half Puerto-Rican? Did you get teased?"

She shrugged. "Honestly, no. I think being from two cultures that have a lot of similarities isn't as challenging as some would say."

I nodded.

"To answer your question, yes, Rita does mean 'pearl' in Spanish and my mother, with all that I remember of her, was the kind of woman that made you feel like you were somebody even if the world said you weren't. I had black friends who would come over and talk to her about their insecurities growing up in America – not feeling like they'd ever have a fair shot because of their skin color. She'd always say how beautiful they were or how much they could change the world like Dr. King."

"So she was a neighborhood activist?"

She laughed. "Yeah. I guess you could say that. It wasn't just for black children, though. She did it for any child who needed encouragement. Some of her black friends would say 'Girl, God certainly gave you somebody else's body, cause you're black.' She would just laugh and wave them off. But she embraced her culture; a lot. Whether it was cooking Spanish dishes or taking me to Puerto Rico when I was five, she learned to make sure that my life had balance. Being Desmond's wife wasn't easy."

I swallowed. I felt like another secret was coming, but I wasn't prepared for it being about my Papa. I could feel my rage surfacing.

"No. Not Papa?" I gasped, faking innocence.

She smirked. "I won't taint your image of our Papa Bear. He wasn't a bad husband. He was just a better father. Much better. I think then, balancing the business at a young age and trying to be a husband was too much. I knew whatever was going on had nothing to do with me. They always assured me of that just by being loving parents."

I shifted in my chair. "So, tell me more about her. I know it was cancer, but how did you guys find out?"

"She collapsed at work," she said quietly. "About six months after we returned from Puerto Rico. She'd been complaining about her stomach bothering her. She hadn't eaten spicy food in a couple of months, so she ruled out acid reflux and heartburn. We were shocked."

She turned and looked out the restaurant window. I followed her eyes across the street, then looked back at her.

She looked down at her hands that were now in her lap, then back at me.

"They used to run together every morning," she continued, her voice now back to normal. "For every unhealthy dish we had, there were five healthy dishes."

"So it made no sense."

"None at all. How could she have gotten cancer? Not one unhealthy bone in her body."

I sighed. I hated talking about illness and death. I looked at my phone. The light was blinking, showing I had a few notifications. I stared at my phone for a few minutes.

"Bre," she continued, leaning up and lightly pulling my face toward her. "I'm sorry. I didn't mean to make you sad."

I sat straight up. "No, no. I'm here for you." I flagged her off. "I had a few notifications. Keep going."

I picked my phone up and checked to see who it was, then put it back down. We tried to be completely present whenever we were together.

"If you have to call someone back, you can."

"Stop trying to avoid the conversation. I'm fine, and you're venting. You need to talk about this."

She smiled. "You definitely have Mama's maturity and selflessness."

I smiled. "Go on."

"Well, the first couple of months were a little challenging. Between the chemo and the radiation, she was losing more than she was winning. In the beginning, she didn't want to do both. She tried the holistic approach and just the chemo, but stomach cancer can spread quickly. And it did."

The tears she'd been fighting fell one by one. I pulled my chair around and put my arm around her. "Emé. It's okay. I'm here."

It was painful seeing her relive her mother's death. If she'd been bottling all this up for that long, there would definitely be more tense days between her and mom than I anticipated.

"A few months after my sixth birthday, she died. It was over, just like that. Not even a whole year with the beast." She sipped her water, and I waited for her to finish. "The little girl who had the baby dolls lined up playing doctor had changed her mind about being a doctor in almost an instant." She snapped her fingers. "Getting a trade was better for me. And then, I got bitten by the acting bug."

"What made you choose skin care as a trade?"

"For one, I knew it would only take a year. I spent one year at Spelman, then dropped out to do the skin care classes. I had a desire to create something for women of color, especially for bi-racial women. During those few years I lived in Atlanta, I auditioned for acting roles whenever I had the chance. My first goal was to get the one-liner. When I did, that one-liner meant everything to me. I studied it like I was the lead. Not finishing college was devastating for daddy. He wanted me to go, but when I showed him my business plan for Empress, he was blown away. He invested in it and everything."

I smiled. "So why get upset that you weren't getting a college degree?"

"Because in his mind, me choosing to focus on building the Empress brand with Noni was supposed to make me focus on something more secure, not acting. So, as proud as he was to see me on screen lighting up the world, he couldn't wait to bring me back to reality with his stats and facts. He just feels acting is too unstable. I never wanted to rely on his resources, so I did what was best for me."

"Papa breathes business, you know that. He just wants us to never have to work for anyone and to show the world that blacks can be financially secure."

She smiled. "And that's where we agree, and I love that about him. My mother loved the same thing. His drive. His push to always make sure she didn't have to work if she didn't want to and to give us the best of everything. Our grandparents played a large role in that, too."

Our paternal grandmother was still living, but our grandfather wasn't.

"He kept me in lots of activities, including dance and theater. And that was where I noticed I had a real talent. My mother told him right before she died, so he ended up investing in my love of the arts. I did play volleyball in high school, but that was just to stay productive."

"Maybe that's why he kept you in theater and acting because he knew it was something she wanted too."

She nodded. "Of course, that's why." A look of longing came over Emé's face. "I wish she could've been there when I graduated from high school; even if it was just to see her smile. Her smile could calm him down in an instant."

"Sounds like your mom and Mama have a lot in common."

"I know they do," she said, looking down again.

It was quiet for a few minutes before she finished. "Between acting and my skin care line, I have something to keep me focused. It's just when the anniversary of her death rolls around, it just seems like I can't get it together."

"Does Derrick help?"

"Yes, he and Noni make things easier."

Our eyes locked for a second. Then, I looked away again. "But not us?"

"Bre. Just because my man and my friends support me doesn't mean I don't need you guys," she said. "Sometimes, family is too close to the situation to help the way I may need it."

She reached out and touched my hand. "Don't you ever doubt that I need you because I do. Period. You mean the world to me and you know that. You're like the daughter I never had."

As soon as she said it, my phone lit up again. I picked it up and noticed it was an email from Paris. I also had a missed text from Desmond.

"Desmond just texted me saying dinner starts promptly at seven. Papa's orders."

❧ ❧ ❧

My mood was ruined after my morning with Emé, that was until I saw Saith.

"I missed you."

It was the first thing Saith said when I walked out into the courtyard. Lunch with Emé was draining, and I hadn't stopped crying since I got back. Once I got myself together, I returned his text and told him to meet me outside. Tonight was the night our families would have dinner together. My parents were out shopping for the food. I turned and looked at Desmond who came out to keep an eye on me. I was just glad he stayed back far enough to let us have a private conversation.

"I missed you, too," I said. "Sorry about all this."

"Don't you dare apologize. I shouldn't have let you push my chair."

I frowned. "Saith, I had pain in my knee long before that day. I was the one who ignored it. I should be apologizing to you." I brushed my hair out of my face. "For scaring you."

134

He rolled his chair closer to me, and I settled down on the edge of the fountain. My father had it cleaned yesterday, so the water was off. It was strange meeting in our usual spot without the gentle sound of flowing water. I couldn't help but wonder if that spoke at all to how our friendship now looked.

"I guess I just realize I can't run from something that wants me," I continued. "No matter what I do, lupus is now my new best friend."

He sighed. "You can't look at it that way. It's not the end of the world, and you know it. You're a fighter. You helped me believe again."

I turned to look at him. A few robins flew around and landed on the tree behind the fountain.

"I wasn't sure I'd ever be able to see life in a good way after losing my mom and my scholarship. I didn't get it and honestly, I still don't."

He touched my hand. I looked over at Desmond who was busy talking on the phone. I relaxed my hand under Saith's.

"But I know that I feel a confidence that I haven't felt in months. Something that I never thought I'd have again."

"That's because you associate what you do with who you are. You don't need to do that."

He gave my hand a little squeeze. "See what I mean. Look how positive you are. You might start off having a bummed day, but you always end up getting your focus back. And that's what I'd lost. My focus."

"So now?"

"I just keep moving forward. I know that I have other gifts and I can work on other things. Basketball doesn't define who I am, it's just one skill set that I have."

A week ago, we had a small dinner at his house. His father had taken Myla to a therapy appointment, so we made good use of the two hours we had. Saith had been gradually improving. I knew he was frustrated that things weren't moving so fast, but his spirits were higher, and he told me he'd been able to move around a little easier.

I laughed and threw my head back. "God, I think he's got it. Give this boy a cookie."

He twisted his lips. "You got jokes, huh?"

I looked at him, and he winked. "My point is, the same way you encouraged me you can encourage yourself. I don't have all the answers."

"God does. Even on my darkest days, He gets me through."

He looked down at his lap. "The jury is still out on that part for me. But I know something great is happening in my life, and I want you there for it."

There they were, the butterflies again. I leaned forward, resting my chin in my hand and looked over at him. I don't know why I was hiding my stomach like he could see what I was feeling.

"Well, that depends on how you can handle the Double D trouble you're about to be faced with."

He chuckled. "The two Desmond's, huh?"

"Yep," I said, staring at my brother again. He was off the phone and was now walking toward us. Saith moved his hand before I had to say anything. I wasn't sure if it was out of respect for my family and me or out of fear. The latter would make me mad.

"Saith, how's it going?" asked Desmond. He shook Saith's hand. "You ready for dinner tonight?"

Saith smiled. "Mentally, I'm ready. I'm not sure if I'll be able to physically do anything."

I laughed. Desmond had a confused look on his face. When he realized what Saith was alluding to, he joined in.

"Listen. We don't have any problems with you, and we don't believe in violence," he said. "We love Brelyn. I think that's understandable. Probably the same way you feel about your cousin Myla."

Saith swallowed. "Yeah, I get it. I never questioned it," he said, never taking his eyes off of Desmond. "What are we having tonight?"

"Well, our parents put together the menu. They should be back shortly," I said.

Desmond put his hand on my shoulder and gave it a little squeeze. "I'm about to go inside in a few minutes. Come in and help your big brother get ready for tonight."

"I don't feel like it," I pushed back. "And you know I'm not going to exert my energy. Doctor's orders."

"It's okay, Bre," Saith said. "Go ahead. We'll talk tonight."

I looked at him. He winked and gave me a little smile. I stood up and bent down to give him a hug. I could feel Desmond's eyes boring a hole in my back.

"I'll see you in a bit," I said. I turned back to Desmond. "Let's go, big bro."

He wrapped his arm around my shoulder, and I wrapped mine around his waist. We headed toward the house.

"Hey, Desmond," Saith called out.

He turned slowly back around. "What's up?"

"Thanks for letting me know there would be no violence," Saith called out with a grin. "My father will be very happy to hear that."

I grinned. One thing I loved about Saith was that he had the ability to make any situation less uncomfortable. I looked up at Desmond and kissed his cheek. He smiled at me, then turned back to Saith.

"I didn't say there wouldn't be any," he said, no longer smiling. "I said we don't believe in it."

I was so embarrassed I couldn't even turn around to wave one last time at Saith. It took Desmond all of ten seconds to let the air out of the cloud I had just been flying on. There was no point in being mad about it because dinner tonight was the real test. I wasn't even sure I was prepared for Double D trouble.

Chapter 15

The conversations at dinner flowed naturally and freely, much to my delight; but I couldn't help but feel like the other shoe was soon to drop.

"And the article about the new Philadelphia International Records studio that's being built? I'm so glad you were able to sit down with Kenny Gamble and his team to capture that story. It means a lot to the culture of Philadelphia," my mother said to Mr. Richards.

We were enjoying the buttery biscuits and seafood macaroni and cheese my mother made as an appetizer. The aroma of teriyaki baked chicken and green bean casserole drifted into the dining room where we sat. I could smell the green peppers that I knew Mama had baked inside the casserole, giving it the extra kick that we all liked. Mr. Richards, Saith and Myla arrived thirty minutes ago. I'd only been able to snag five minutes with him before Papa walked into the foyer and invited them all into the living room.

After a short talk there, Mama called us into the dining room, where she and Mr. Richards were discussing the latest issue of Urban Central magazine. The cover story was about one of Philadelphia's legends, Kenny Gamble, and his legacy.

"It was a great write up," Papa chimed in. "I think I may know the writer. Is that the same Stacey McQueen who used to work for the New York Times?"

"Sure is," Mr. Richards said, biting into another biscuit. "She's been with me for the last six months. Amazing writer." He turned to Mama. "These biscuits are amazing. Did I hear you say that you made these from scratch?"

"I did," Mama said.

I saw Papa staring at Mr. Richards. I had to chuckle. Mama was giving Papa a look that told him his dessert was one of a kind, yet he still couldn't resist looking at Mr. Richards like he was chopped liver while he talked to Mama. I was glad when Mr. Richards turned back to Papa.

"Sorry about that," he said, licking his finger. "I know that's classless, but those biscuits are to die for. But, yes, Stacey. Amazing writer. You know her?"

"That's how she got me," Papa said, winking. "Those biscuits."

"I thought you said it was her smile, Pop," Desmond chimed in.

Everyone laughed. "Desmond, mind yours," Papa said. "It was everything. That's why we've been married for seventeen years."

Mama placed another bowl on the table just as Papa grabbed her around the waist. He kissed her cheek. "Love you."

She finished placing the main dishes on the table. "Love you more," she said. "Alright. Cashmere, put the phone down before I trash it. Desmond, grab the lemonade from the fridge.

Bre," she said, walking over to me. "I want you to relax. Okay?"

She planted a kiss on my forehead. I looked at Papa, and he made a face at me. I smiled.

"Emé just texted me. She's ten minutes away," Cashmere said.

I looked down at my phone. Sure enough, I had a missed text message from Emé. *See you soon, baby girl.* I didn't realize I had zoned out reading her text message until Desmond came over and touched me gently on the back. He leaned down and whispered in my ear.

"I see you didn't give your boyfriend a kiss tonight," he said. "He looks so sad."

I pinched him before he had a chance to run away. He stopped at Saith's wheelchair. "Listen, man, be yourself. Just be careful."

"Papa!" I screamed out. Desmond was starting his big brother tactics before dinner was even underway.

Papa just stood there and smiled. "What did he do?" he said, faking innocence.

I gave them both death stares. Cashmere walked over and hugged me from behind. "Welcome to my world," she whispered, taking her seat.

"Okay," she continued. "Everything's on the table. Myla, mom doesn't allow cellphones at the dinner table, so you'll have to put that away."

I watched as Myla looked up slowly at Cashmere, then at Mr. Richards. He nodded. She put the phone in her purse. I caught Cashmere's eyes, and she raised an eyebrow. I wondered what would've happened had Mr. Richards not given her the nod. Everyone settled into their seats. Desmond moved over one, so Saith could pull his chair in next to me.

Just as we all grabbed hands to say grace, Emé walked in. She moved Cashmere over and grabbed both our hands. We all looked at her. I looked over at her seat next to Mama.

"I'm just standing here for grace. Go, Papa."

He stared at her, then bowed his head. "Heavenly Father, we thank you for being who you are. I pray this dinner is blessed. We invite you into this moment. Thank you for family and potential friends. In Jesus name, Amen."

Just as promised, Emé took her seat next to Mama, kissing her before grabbing her plate.

"Desmond, how do you know Stacey?" Mr. Richards asked as soon as everyone started digging in.

"She did a few write ups on my business over the years," Papa said. Then he looked down at Saith. "Saith, tell me more about yourself. You'll be a senior next year. What are your plans?"

Saith and I were holding hands under the table. He brought his hand back up to the table.

"It depends at this point," he said. "I was blessed to get a guaranteed scholarship while still in my junior year. My injury may have changed some of that, but my choices are Cornell, USC or Temple."

Papa nodded. "Don't let the scholarship deter you. Unlike a lot of people, you have options."

Saith took some food in his mouth. "Yeah. I know we have the money to pay for college, but I fought hard for my basketball scholarship. I don't want to rely on my father's money."

Papa smiled. "A man who works hard and doesn't rest on his inheritance. I love it."

Mama popped Papa's hand. "No business talk tonight."

"I'm talking about my daughter's business with this young man. I didn't say anything about Roger Frances wine," he said back, never taking his eyes off of Saith. "So you and Brelyn like each other?"

"Yes, sir," he said.

"Do people call you junior, so there's no confusion who they're addressing?" Myla asked Desmond, interrupting PaPa's interrogation of Saith.

I wanted to kiss her for that beautiful segue.

"Well, in our family, it's just 'Des' for me and 'Pop' or 'Papa' for our father," he said. "But outside, people just call me Des and him Desmond. I don't like Junior."

"He never did," Emé said, winking at him. "We used to tease him with that name all the time growing up. As soon as he turned twelve, we gave him his respect and called him Des as he wished."

We laughed at the memory.

"Yeah, yeah," he said, wiping at his mouth. "Saith, you got it easy. You only have one woman to live with."

Everyone started chattering and giggling, keeping up the small talk. I noticed Saith got quiet. I touched his arm, and he looked at me. I smiled when he moved my hair out of my face. When I took my eyes off him, my eyes locked with Papa's. I slowly removed my hand from Saith's arm. Papa looked at Mama and smiled. She flirted with him as they tapped their wine glasses together.

"Saith," Emé said, sipping her wine. "I'm sorry about your mother. Do you mind me asking what happened to her?"

It was no secret that Saith's mother was deceased. With his father's high profile magazine and him being an athlete, that part wasn't a secret. I never told anyone that Saith was behind the wheel that night. I'm not even sure the world knew that part. I have no idea how his father was able to keep it all out of the media, but money and great publicists helped.

"Emé, honey, I'm sure Saith doesn't want to relive that night," Mama said. Everyone was quiet now. Emé took a look at Saith's wheelchair and swallowed.

"I'm sorry," she continued. "I didn't realize..."

"Emé's an actress, so she usually spends months at a time on a set or in another city," Mama continued. "Regular news doesn't always make its way to her phone."

Emé glared at Mama. "Well, I keep my CNN alerts on," she said through gritted teeth.

I could feel the tension at my end of the table. "Uh, listen, it's no big deal. I don't think Saith or Mr. Richards want to relive that moment. Why don't you tell us about the upcoming movie release with Christian Leroy, Emé?" I said, my eyes pleading with her to move on.

She stuffed some more food in her mouth. I sighed, relieved. For the next hour, we all ate and made small talk. I enjoyed the moment, knowing Papa would have a personal talk with Saith before he left if he didn't get a chance to ask him anything else right now.

"This was good. Thanks so much, Mrs. Clover," Myla said, slowly taking her phone back out her bag. "May I go next door now?"

"Myla. Relax. We'll all go home when it's time," Saith responded.

Mr. Richards twitched in his seat. "Myla, why don't you tell everyone what you've been working on. I'm excited for you."

She looked at him and then at Saith. "I don't even know them," she said, looking around at everyone. She powered her phone back on. "That's why I need to get back home, I have something to finish by a certain time."

She stared at Mr. Richards. All eyes were on them.

"Dad, just let her go. We won't be much longer," Saith said.

Mr. Richards gave in. "Okay."

She stood up. "Thanks again, everyone. I'll see you guys later," she said.

As soon as we all heard the front door shut, Mr. Richards spoke. "I'm sorry about that," he said. "Myla's been having a rough time dealing with her aunt's death."

"Just out of curiosity," Papa said. "Where are her parents?"

I closed my eyes in embarrassment. "Papa."

He looked at me.

Mr. Richards held his hand up. "It's okay, Brelyn. Myla moved in with us when she was eight. Her mother, my late wife's sister, is deceased and she never knew her father."

I knew that more questions were coming, but I was just praying Mr. Richards and Saith wouldn't be offended. My family had this way of prodding, always with good intentions. I can't remember one time they were nosy and didn't end up helping someone.

"Well, she has you and Saith, and that's all that matters. Two people that love her very much," Mama said.

Emé put her wine glass down and looked at Mama. "That's not all that matters. Is that what you really think? That because someone has a replacement parent or family that the way they feel doesn't matter?" she said. She turned to Saith. "Tell your cousin I know exactly how she feels and if she ever needs someone to talk to, I'm here."

Papa slammed his hand on the table. "Emé. That's enough, dammit."

She flinched but didn't blink. "I just bet it is. No need in your skeletons coming out of the closet since you've exposed theirs."

Saith looked at me. I shook my head.

"What is it?" he whispered. "Why is she so angry?"

"It's nothing," I said, not looking at him. I hadn't told him anything about Emé because it was none of his business. I guess Emé wasn't as concerned about her personal business the way I was.

"Uh, maybe we should go," Mr. Richards said, standing up.

"No, sit," Papa said. "Emé's done. Right, Emé?"

She was seething. She looked back and forth between Mama and Papa, then she looked at all of us. I'd never seen Cashmere this quiet. Ever. I think this was the first time any of us had witnessed Emé acting this way. It left us all speechless. Between her busy schedule and her 'I can do it all mentality,' this was the first time in years we'd experienced her vulnerability. A vulnerability tied to her truth. She turned to Saith.

"Whatever happened, I pray that you get the help you need and that nobody pushes your feelings under the rug."

I knew Papa wasn't going to let that slide.

"*I* pushed your feelings under the rug?" he boomed.

Mama stood up. "Not now," she screamed before either of them could say anything else. She looked at Mr. Richards, who was still standing. He hadn't budged. Saith was looking between Emé and me, trying to figure out what was going on. I smiled weakly.

"I'll FaceTime you later," I said.

"Not now, Emé," Papa said, walking over to Mr. Richards. "The purpose of this dinner was for us to get to know each other better since our children like each other."

"I have no problem with that. I want you to feel safe with Brelyn coming over just as I want to feel the same with my boy visiting you," he said.

Papa squinted his eyes. "Safe? Why wouldn't he be safe over here?"

"I would ask the same with your daughter. It seems we all have issues that need to be worked through," he said. "Unless there's a reason I should be concerned."

"I'm concerned because a sixteen-year-old boy likes my fifteen-year-old daughter. Didn't you just run an article about an athlete who lost his scholarship because he slept with an underage girl? I would think you'd understand that I was thinking of both of them," Papa said.

"Papa, I'm not having sex with Saith. What are you talking about?" I squealed.

Mama walked over and stood in between them. Desmond stood up and walked over to the other side of Papa. Mr. Richards looked back and forth between the two men.

"Listen. I knew what to expect here. I would feel the same way if Myla brought some boy home that was older than her and they liked each other," he said. "What I don't like is that we as men, who both have wonderful legacy's, couldn't sit down and talk about this without tearing each other down. There's no need for the animosity, but I won't be disrespected."

Papa took a few deep breaths. He looked at Saith, then back at Mr. Richards. Cashmere was standing behind me with her hands resting on my shoulders.

"I wasn't trying to disrespect you or your family. She's my baby girl," Papa said. "I want them both to be careful because the world doesn't make it easy for us as it is. One mistake could cost him. One mistake could cost her. I'm already on the edge of my seat with her having lupus."

Mr. Richards put his hand on Papa's shoulder. "My son is paralyzed from the waist down. I lost my wife, and he lost some of his life all in one day. I know how you feel. Trust me. But we have to build each other up. That's what our parents taught us, yes?"

I started smiling again. The Richards family was a lot like ours. They'd both come up in the grit and grime of their cities, only to beat the odds and come out on top. I watched as they shook hands and hugged. My brother smiled and joined in.

"When black men unite," he said, causing us to laugh.

Cashmere hugged me and kissed my cheek. "I'll start cleaning off the table. Emé, help me please sis," she said.

Emé had zoned out; I wasn't even sure she heard Cashmere. The tension between the fathers had grown thick. We didn't know what was about to happen and I wasn't sure I wanted to even witness it. I was just glad Mr. Richards had a backbone and Papa had a soft spot; otherwise things would've been a whole lot messier. Emé started gathering the dishes. She caught my eye and pulled me to the side.

"You okay?" she asked.

I shrugged. "I knew what to expect. He's our father. I just didn't know what Mr. Richards was going to say," I whispered.

"Yeah, well, that's Papa. Ready to set the record straight before someone even says anything."

I swallowed. "Saith isn't that bad."

She shrugged. "In Papa's eyes, any boy that likes his daughters are bad. Even I understand that Bre," she said, walking the bowls in her hand to the kitchen.

When I turned back around, Saith was rolling his chair over to me. "We need to talk," he said.

I nodded, knowing that he would ask all the questions I wasn't sure I wanted to answer. My loyalty to my family was much stronger than my like for Saith, but the fluttering in my stomach was speaking louder than my loyalty right now.

❈ ❈ ❈

Back in my room, I tapped away on the computer, submitting one of my final papers for class and relieved to be sitting at my desk once again. I had to sit up in the bed for the last two weeks after the doctor had given me permission to return to my room. Now that I had full clearance to be out of bed, it was back to business. June was rapidly approaching, and I was ready for summer break. I wasn't sure what I was planning to do, but I knew I had to convince Mama and Papa to let me run my business in some way.

Just as I was opening another email from Paris, Saith FaceTimed me. I'd ignored his first call, and now that it was almost midnight, I wondered if I should take this one. There was no school tomorrow so I couldn't use the excuse that I had to get up. I answered before I could give myself another excuse not to.

"I was about to hang up," he said.

"Yeah. I know," I said. "I just submitted my final for English."

"Good stuff. How do you think you did?"

"Pretty good, I'm sure I'll finish strong," I said. I grabbed my brush and my scarf. "How's the rest of your evening going?"

"It's the next day, Bre," he said sullenly.

"Well, in like three minutes," I teased, brushing my hair.

He was playing around on his laptop, so he was only looking at me occasionally. "I knew your father would hate me, regardless of what I said or did," he said, laughing. "But I wasn't expecting Emé to be so cool."

I hesitated before responding. "Emé didn't mean anything by what she said. I hope you know that." I looked up at the screen. I could see him shifting around. He disappeared for a second, then his face came back into view.

"That's what I wanted to ask you. What was she talking about?"

I looked away from the screen for a second, then back at it. He was fishing.

"It's a long story. One that Emé doesn't even talk much about. Family stuff."

"I get that. She's not your mom's daughter, right?"

That was no secret. "Correct."

Whatever Saith was about to say next was interrupted by an email I received. When my computer chimed, I opened the email while keeping my FaceTime screen up.

"I just got an email. Give me a second," I said.

"This late?"

I skimmed the email quickly. "Yeah. It's from the client I was telling you about. She's here visiting family in Philly."

He looked at me. "Was that planned?"

"Yes. She knew she was coming to visit family the end of this month." I saw him pause. "What Saith?"

"Nothing. I thought you said your parents wanted you to take a break from your business for a minute."

I rolled my eyes. "They did. You gonna snitch on me?

He grunted. "Never. I just want you to be careful. That's all. How do you know Paris isn't some guy? That's a unisex name, ya know?"

I raised an eyebrow. "You jealous?"

"No. Do I have a reason to be?"

My stomach was fluttering again. "No," I said, giving Saith my full attention. "I know my father spoke to you after dinner. What did he say?"

"So now we're telling all?"

I caught his sarcasm. "My family issues are none of your concern. What my father says to you about *us* is my concern."

I knew he wouldn't be pleased with the answer.

"You know Bre, I never talk about what happened with my mother, ever. But I felt comfortable enough telling you."

I sighed. "And I'm here to support you through that, but your situation is different. That was about you. Ask me anything about me, and I'm an open book."

He scrunched his face up. After a few seconds of silence, he spoke. "You're right. I never looked at it that way. So, Brelyn Michele Clover, do you like me enough to talk your dad out of sitting in on all our dates?"

My eyes grew wide. "They couldn't even let me tell you that part, huh?"

Saith started laughing, but I was seething. "They also said, you couldn't date until your senior year."

"You're kidding?" I asked, standing.

He held his hands up and shook his head. "I'm just kidding. Relax." Once I sat back down, he continued. "He has to get to know me. I've been through this before with other girls, Bre."

I could tell by the way he bit his lip and looked down that he didn't mean to say that.

"Must've been a lot of girls?" I quipped.

I typed away a response to Paris on my computer. She wanted to meet next Saturday evening. Getting out on the weekend would be tougher than getting out during the week. Dr. Warhol came by on the weekends. He showed up every Friday at five like clockwork. It helped me get recharged for the week ahead, but he didn't usually leave until Sunday evening. He stayed in one of our guestrooms over the weekend. Getting out on a Saturday evening would be a huge challenge with him there. Although he encouraged being a "normal" teen, I was sure that didn't mean going out and meeting with a client. I had to think of something.

"Bre, you still with me?" Saith said.

I smiled. "Yeah. Just let me reply to this email."

I heard a knock at my door. Without me saying anything, I knew it was Cashmere. She knocked two times, paused, then knocked again.

"What's up, Cash?"

She opened it. "You better get some rest, sis. You need anything to help you sleep? Did you take your meds?"

"No and yes; and I'm about to go to sleep."

She looked at my computer screen. A smile inched its way across her face. "Don't get boy crazy like me," she said, winking. I smiled at her.

"Never," I said, winking. "Night sis. Love you."

"Love you more," she said.

When she left, I turned back to Saith. "I gotta go. We'll talk tomorrow."

I blew him a little kiss. He playfully caught it.

"Good night," he said. There was an undertone of sadness in his voice. I wasn't sure whether it was because I didn't tell him more about Emé or that I had to hang up. Either way, business and sleep were both calling me. I had to go. Waving bye, I ended our FaceTime call.

I hit reply on Paris's email:

Hi Paris,

Face to face consultations are sixty dollars an hour and include a follow-up email with a customized plan. I will get back to you and let you know if I have an available appointment on Saturday. If not, please let me know the best days and times that you can meet during your visit. I hope you enjoy your stay in Philly.

Best, Brelyn M. Clover

Chapter 16

The rest of the week flew by and soon I was once again face to face with Dr. Warhol.

"You have to drink all the water that you can," he said, "in addition to the Gatorade. Stay hydrated."

Nothing he said made much sense to me since I drank mostly water. I sat there as he finished examining me, waiting for him to finish. I was typing away on my laptop, moving it around as he needed me to.

"Brelyn, whatever homework you're doing I'm sure can wait," Mama said.

I looked at her. "I finished my homework already."

She crossed her arms. "What is so important then that you can't wait until Dr. Warhol is done examining you?"

I bit my bottom lip. "Just some things I want to work on." I realized then, I should've kept my mouth shut. "Dr. Warhol mentioned last time that it was a good idea for me to keep a journal," I said quickly before she could ask another question.

He nodded, lifting my right leg slightly. "She's correct. The laptop is fine. I can work around it."

I giggled at his accent. "I love your accent."

He made a face and then smiled. "It's my special feature," he replied as laid his accent on extra thick.

Mama relaxed and smiled herself. "Just let us know what else she needs, and we'll get it."

She'd already said that a million times since he'd shown up, but I just continued typing, not even paying attention to what he was saying. Truth be told, I was writing. It wasn't necessarily a journal like Dr. Warhol had suggested, but rather a few notes I wanted to keep for my business. I quickly opened a new Word document and typed today's date, scribbling a few lines about my health. I was already doing research on nutrition so nothing would seem odd there.

"Dr. Warhol," I said. "Is there any way I can hang out this weekend? Like just for a few hours?"

I figured it was better to ask than to sneak and cause unnecessary confusion. I had four human guard dogs to be worried about, not to mention Saith. There was no way I would make it out the house without some kind of twenty-page questionnaire from both parents and my siblings.

"I don't think that's a good idea," Mama said.

"I'm asking Dr. Warhol. If he says I'm healthy enough to do it, then I should be fine."

I immediately looked away when I saw the look on Mama's face. I lowered my tone. "I just think we should let the doctor say what he thinks before jumping to conclusions, Mama. He is the expert."

She looked at me intently but didn't say anything. Dr. Warhol looked in between Mama and me before speaking again.

"Mrs. Clover, Brelyn can go out and hang with her friends. Brelyn just has to listen to her body. If she's walking for a long period of time and gets tired, she needs to rest. If she feels any throbbing, she needs to rest. If any pain persists for more than an hour, she needs to come home. Everything seems neutralized for now, and she is still very healthy," he said, pushing his glasses up on his nose. "I think you keep forgetting that she is human. Until Brelyn tells you there's a problem or that's she's experiencing pain, don't deprive her of having a normal life."

I looked at Mama, proud that I held the trump card. If he was saying it was okay, then I could email Paris back about meeting tomorrow afternoon. She had landed on this past Wednesday and would be leaving on Monday.

"Did you hear what he said, Brelyn?" Mama said. "He said as long as you rest when you feel pain and come home if it persists. That means you need to communicate and not hold it all in." She looked at Dr. Warhol. "That's been her problem lately. She doesn't seem to take this serious."

"Now, Brelyn, I must say that your father warned me about how stubborn the Clover women could be," Dr. Warhol said.

Mama cleared her throat. He looked at her apologetically. "Well, he was speaking of the Clovers in general. Anyway, this isn't a cold. As much as it may have shocked you and even frightened you, you can't play around with this. As long as you continue to eat healthily, take your medications and stick close to your doctor—"

"And family," Mama interrupted.

"And family, you'll be fine."

I waited until they finished. I turned the computer toward him. The open tab that I had up on my computer to the WebMD website. "Is this true?" I asked, pointing to the second paragraph. "That seventy percent of people live twenty years after their diagnosis?"

Mama dropped her arms to her side and started walking toward me. I put my hand up, never taking my eyes off the doctor. "Is it?"

He looked down at his hands. When he looked back up, he took his glasses off. "That's just a statistic, and you have to remember, you have a milder case of lupus. Follow my instructions, and you'll have the best outcomes possible. We've gone over this before."

As tears sprang to my eyes, I looked back at Mama. "I know we have. I know the numbers. I read all the brochures, and I even have the stupid 'L' for lupus hanging up in my room." I slammed the laptop shut. "I didn't show you guys this because I forgot. I showed you because I want to *live* my life for however long I'm going to be here."

After my checkup with Dr. Warhol, I was happy when Saturday morning rolled around. Last night, Mama stayed by my bedside the whole night, only getting up to refill the water pitcher. I only asked her if I could hang in Olde City for a few hours. The problem was, I had to get Saith on board. I sat up and opened my laptop. I wanted to walk upstairs to my room, but I didn't want to wait too long. Saith usually went to rehab on Saturdays. Ever since he'd linked with his physical therapist, our sessions had ended. That didn't stop us from getting closer, though.

"Hey, sweets," he said, picking up my FaceTime call on the first ring. "Can't talk long. I'm about to finish my session."

"I see you're working hard. Anymore sweat, and I'll feel it through the phone."

He was drenched. A part of me liked seeing him like that.

"I can't wait to give you a big sweaty hug when I see you," he said, sticking his tongue out. He turned to his therapist. "Bre, this is Lindsay. She says I have to go."

"Hi, Brelyn," Lindsay said, coming into camera view. "He talks about you all the time."

I grinned. Saith looked down in his lap. "I do not."

I frowned. "I'm sure you don't," I teased. "I need a favor." When Lindsay walked away, I continued. "I'm meeting up with Paris this afternoon at three. We're meeting downtown in Olde City at Third and Market."

Saith wiped his forehead. "Okay. You want me to come with you? I'm not sure I'll be done in time, but I can meet you there."

I hadn't thought about that, but that would work perfectly. "That works. Come after. It's only for an hour since that's all she's paying me for. I don't want to do business with someone else sitting there. It's not professional."

He sighed. "Bre, you're meeting someone you've never met before. You need to take someone with you."

"Why? If I weren't sick and running my fitness classes, I'd have consultations all the time," I said, defensively.

"I told you about doing that," he responded. "This has nothing to do with your sickness. All I'm saying is you need to be careful. Your classes were filled with members that you said either you or your parents knew. Isn't that what you told me?"

He was getting upset. I didn't mean to piss him off, especially during his session. I knew he only had a few more minutes, so I softened up.

"Listen, I apologize for that," I said, bringing the laptop closer to my face. I pouted. "How about you meet me there, say around 3:30? We'll meet at the coffee shop on the corner. That'll make it easier. They have the wheelchair accessibility."

He smiled. "Okay. Our first real date, huh?"

"Without my parents," I said. "I'll have to convince them that it'll be fine, but I know they'll want Cashmere or Desmond to tag along."

"Wait, wait," he said. "So they have no idea you're meeting this girl?"

I closed my eyes. Epic fail. Saith was worried enough about my parents and Desmond. I put my foot in my mouth, but I knew the only way to get him on my side was to tell him the truth. If I was going to rebel, I needed to have at least one solid ally who I could trust.

"Saith, the one thing that's keeping me sane right now is Psalm twenty-three and my business," I said, tears welling up in my eyes. "And you. I need you to help me with this. I'm trying to do everything that everyone else wants me to do, but my business is mine. It's my baby."

I hated that I was crying in front of someone I liked this much. However, in the two months I'd known Saith, he made my me feel that I could trust him with my tears.

"I have to go. Lindsay only gave me a ten-minute break, and I'm already over by two minutes. She has another appointment after me," he said. "I have your back, and that includes making sure you're doing what's best for your health; not just what you want to do?"

"Yes," I said. "So, how about we do it together?"

He frowned. "What? Run your business?"

"Listen. Meet me today at three thirty. We can discuss it more after Paris leaves. But, it could work. Maybe as a consultant. I just need you to screen everyone."

He looked over and gave Lindsay the one-minute finger. "I have to go. I promise I'll be there at three thirty We'll talk then."

I nodded. "See ya."

159

"Wait," he said. "Bre?"

"Yeah."

"Be careful. I can't lose you too."

❀ ❀ ❀

When I walked inside *Grinded Effort* coffee shop, I looked around for Paris. I was wearing my purple and blue fitness set with a matching baseball cap. It felt good to be back in fitness gear after being out of it for almost three weeks. As I walked to the counter to buy an iced coffee, I looked at the calendar hanging near the register. There were only two days left in May.

"Thank you," the cashier said. "I hope you don't mind me asking you this, but aren't you that girl whose father owns the winery? I saw your story in Forbes."

I forced a smile. Nice time for me to try to be low-key. I stuck my hand out to introduce myself. "Brelyn. Nice to meet you..." I looked at her name tag, "Kensey."

She smiled. "Nice to meet you, too. My professor brought the article in for my Business and Ethics class; he loves the way your father does business."

I grinned. At least this was a good review. "I appreciate that. I'm actually waiting to meet with someone. Tell your professor thanks."

I wanted to hand her a business card, but I technically wasn't there on business, and I wanted to keep it that way. When Mama saw me putting my fitness gear on, I had to come up with the story of all stories, which was only partially a lie.

"Mama, Saith is meeting me there. I know you and Papa said I couldn't date alone, but Desmond is working on one of his designs with his team and Cashmere is with Emé for the weekend. Papa's away at a conference, and you have to prepare for your meeting with the jeweler on Monday. My life shouldn't have to stop and wait for everyone else's."

I knew I was wrong for laying the guilt trip on her, but between our talk with the doctor and my constant reminder that holding me back would only make me want to do it more, she gave in. We made a deal that it was our little secret, and I was not to tell Papa that she let me go. She also stressed that this was a one-time thing. Period. I settled down at a table near the front door, just in case Paris did turn out to be psycho I could easily dash out. Plus, Saith would be able to see me. I chuckled at the thought of running from a girl who claimed to be obese. In reality, she was in no way obese. Sadly, her views on her body stemmed from society's perpetuated need to be thin.

I had to admit, some things seemed a bit odd. I knew getting out of school in May wasn't unusual, but why she needed to travel all the way to Philadelphia to meet with a fitness expert was beyond me. Papa always taught me that when people believed in you, they would invest in you. While I'd like to think that my story was amazing and inspiring, I was sure Atlanta has plenty of trainers she could've chosen from. I texted Saith to let him know I was there safe and he texted back that he would be here by three thirty as promised. My phone rang just as a girl that looked like Paris walked into the shop. I glared at her as she walked to the counter, but I didn't say anything.

"Mama, I made it safely," I said, answering on the third ring.

"Okay, tell Saith I said to be careful and to call me if you experience any pain. Matter of fact, let me talk to him."

My heart started beating fast. "He isn't here yet. He just texted me and said he was a few minutes away. I told you we were meeting here after his therapy session."

That part was true.

"And I told you," she said sternly, "when I dropped you off at the train station, that you needed to time it so that he was there first. Did I not say that? So what time will he be there?"

I looked up just as Paris turned around. She had a latte in her hand. It was indeed her. She waved and started walking over. I stood up in a rush, knocking over my own iced drink.

"Damn," I said. I immediately covered my mouth, hoping that the smoke that I was sure was coming from Mama's ears would've blocked her from hearing me. "Mama, I just spilled my drink all over the table and on someone's bag. I'm fine. He'll be here shortly." I took the phone away. "Ma'am, sorry about that. Give me a second. I gotta go, Mama. Love you. Call you in a few."

I hung up. Though I'd never hung up before my mother finished her last statement, I was glad I had. Paris just reached the table, and some of the iced coffee *had* spilled onto a bag that was on the floor. It belonged to the guy next to me. I grabbed napkins from nearby as the girl from behind the register came over with a mop. Paris stood to the side.

"You okay?" she asked.

I nodded, trying to maintain my cool. "Sorry about that, sir. Your next coffee's on me."

He didn't move but said a quick "Thanks" as he helped me wipe his bag off. I could sense his irritation.

"No worries, Brelyn," Kensey said, mopping the floor. "I got it."

As she mopped up my mess, Paris and I moved over to the next table. Thankfully, it was also close enough to the door that Saith could see me when he got here. I handed Kensey a ten-dollar bill.

"For his next coffee and your tip," I said.

She grinned wildly as she walked back to the counter. I was relieved that I'd only brought my tablet and that it was still in my bag.

"Well, how are you?" Paris said, taking off her hat. "It's nice to finally meet you."

"You also," I said. "You look exactly like your picture."

I hadn't meant to say that out loud, but she did. Usually, there was some kind of difference, whether the person had on extra makeup or their face looked chubbier, that wasn't the case with Paris. I prepared for our consultation, by setting up my tablet and preparing to take notes. It was just two fifty-five. My phone chimed. I knew it had to be Mama. I sent her a quick text. *Everything's fine. I am going to call you in a little bit. Love you.* It wasn't like I could text Papa to calm her down. It was our secret. I put my phone on vibrate and turned to Paris.

"So, let's get started. Do you have the questionnaire I sent you?"

She nodded and pulled it out of her bag. It was a cute, large pink and gold shoulder bag.

"Nice bag," I said, grabbing the papers.

"You typed in your answers?" I asked, looking at her.

"It's the nerd in me," she giggled. "Brelyn, I just really wanted to thank you for everything. This is the closest I've been to achieving my goal."

I sat back and looked at her. Before saying anything, I took a quick glance over her answers.

"Just out of curiosity," I started. "You mentioned that you came to America when you were four in our emails, but your questionnaire says twelve. That would be just four years ago. You're sixteen, right?"

She nodded. "My family moved here when I was twelve. The first time I came was when I was four," she said, sipping her latte. "It's a long story. Mainly, a lot of back and forth between my parents."

I flipped to the next page and continued reading. "Please don't take this the wrong way, but your English is great for someone who hasn't lived here that long. Did you have an ESL tutor?"

She sighed. "Education is very important in my family. I learned a lot in India, then when we settled here, my parents provided me with a private tutor for home-study."

I nodded. I finished skimming the papers and pulled up my consultation questionnaire. I had twenty minutes before Saith would arrive. The plan was for him to just come in and ignore me, but sit in another corner so he could come over when Paris and I were done. For the next twenty minutes, I took notes on the goals Paris was trying to achieve. The original three-day option I'd given her had been working, so she wanted to up the ante. I pushed the gnawing feeling that something was wrong to the back of my mind. The details about her weight and what she was hoping to achieve were fine. It was her family background that came off sketchy. I put if off that she was just as reluctant as I was to meet with someone from the internet and didn't want to share all the details of her life.

I, for one, knew how that felt. Although my family was well known, it was always a challenge for me to open up to anyone that I didn't know well. I was a bit uncomfortable as I listened to Paris speak about the Forbes story on my family because she spoke as if she knew us. She never once *asked* me questions regarding me or Bodies by Brelyn. It was a bit weird, but I had to believe what she was being genuine, just like I hoped she'd decided to believe in me. My vibrating bag pulled me from my thoughts. I peeked at the phone inside my bag to see Saith's name pop up. *He's here*, I thought.

"Well, I know we have until four, but could you excuse me for a minute? I have another client at four, and they just texted me."

The smile faded from Paris' face. "I didn't know you had another appointment. I thought you said you had to rush back home immediately."

I couldn't remember what I'd told her. I looked at her. I was trying to figure out what part of this consultation required her to know my whereabouts after the one hour she'd paid for.

"Well, our meeting ends at four. Theirs starts at four fifteen, but I like to mentally prepare. But, you paid for an hour, and that's all that matters," I said, standing up. "I'll extend it to five after for having to respond to this text, but an hour is an hour," I finished, smiling brightly.

After seeing Saith roll in, I responded: *All is going well. You can come over at five after four. Don't wait for her to leave. You're my next appointment.*

"Is that your next client?" she asked, pointing at Saith. She looked back at me just as I put my phone away. "He's cute."

I relaxed. "Yep, he's focused on regaining his strength," I said, picking up my tablet again. "So, here's what I'd like to do. I know you're only here for the next few days—"

"No. My parents extended the stay," she interrupted. "I'll be here until next Saturday. My aunt needs my mother's help."

I peered at her from over my tablet. Without showing a change in my facial expression, I continued. "Okay. Well, let me finish going over my suggestions, and we'll take it from there."

This girl needs to relax. She's too high strung.

"I have all the details I need based on everything we just went over. What I'd like to do is make sure you can stick to an extended, one-month plan. I'll go over a few different kits and see which one would be best to send to you based on the healthy foods you enjoy eating most. I noticed that people get more mileage out of eating healthy when they eat foods they enjoy."

"I tell my parents that all the time. As long as I can have broccoli with butter, I am happy. Nothing else."

I laughed. "I understand that. I have restrictions on my own diet, so my favorite green veggies are spinach, broccoli and cucumbers."

Her face softened. "Do you find yourself ever feeling scared to die?"

I felt a chill travel up my spine. I shuddered. Papa had always taught us to keep business and personal separate. In this situation, my personal was now a part of my business. It was why so many people were encouraging me so much and I loathed the idea, but I responded anyway.

"My doctor and I were discussing that the other day," I said. "The truth is I have no idea how long I'll be here. But while I am here, I'm going to be the best fitness and health guru I can be. With that, I'm thankful to have you onboard." *Great segue*, I thought. "I'm glad you didn't see my health as a hindrance. Once I go over a few plans, hopefully you'll see that I can help you."

She smiled. "How much do the one-month plans start at?"

I hit a button on my tablet and set it up in front of her. "See, here are the ones that seem to fit your lifestyle best," I said. "They start from three hundred dollars and go up to seven hundred and fifty dollars. However, I can customize one according to your budget."

She frowned. "That's pretty steep. I'm not even sure I could afford the consultation and the three-day plan you gave me."

"I completely understand. Don't worry. That's why a consultation is to let you see what options you can choose from. It does include a one-page customized 'Get Started' plan, but it's just a summary of what we discussed and ideas to move forward. To see real results, you'll need to purchase a plan."

Paris nodded. "I'll have to go over it and let you know. I think I can do it if my parents can see the improvements it'll make." She bit her bottom lip and paused before speaking again. "They are very concerned with my health."

I glanced up at the clock. It was three-fifty-five. I looked up to see Kensey taking off her apron.

"Well, I'll send you the one-page summary no later than tomorrow morning. I want to give you the last ten minutes to ask any questions you may have?"

She took out her phone. "Yes. I wanted to know the name of the doctor you were seeing." I raised an eyebrow. "I only asked because my father has a friend who studies Rheumatology, he may be able to help you."

I appreciated the gesture, but it was weird for her to say she didn't have much money to pay for my services, yet waste her last ten minutes to ask me about a doctor. Without having to say his name, I was sure she knew my family had no problems paying for the best.

"Dr. Warhol is one of the best in the country. He's on our personal staff, and I know my father went through the extremes of making sure he was the best," I said. "Did you have any questions about your weight loss goals?"

She forced a smile. "I apologize. I wasn't trying to pry. I appreciate you even meeting with me. I don't have any questions right this second. Maybe I'll have some after I go over the plans and I'll I need a few days to do that." Paris said with what seemed like a forced smile. "Is it okay if I email them to you?" she asked.

"Sure, you can do that," I said, relieved that she'd gotten the picture.

"Maybe we could help each other," she said, putting her hat back on. It was a cute pink beret to match her bag. "I may not be able to purchase a plan until late June, but I would love to keep in touch."

"I don't mind tweeting and emailing," I said, looking up. Saith was making his way over.

Paris turned around just as he was moving the chair next to our table. She stuck her hand out. "I'm Paris. We were just wrapping up."

He shook it. "Saith. Nice to meet you, Paris. I'm not rushing you guys. It just takes me a minute to maneuver this thing."

She nodded. I noticed she was still holding onto his hand. Saith looked at me and quickly pulled his hand away. I raised my eyebrow.

"I appreciate your time, Paris," I said. "Give me a day to send you the summary. I'm sure if you keep using the three-day plan as a guide, you'll be fine until you can afford something more consistent."

I stuck my hand out and was surprised when she reached in for a hug. I wasn't rude, so I hugged her back. "Thanks, Brelyn. I'll be in touch." Just then her phone rang. "Yes. I'm coming outside now," she said, hanging up. "See you guys later."

Saith and I both watched as she went outside and got into a silver car with tinted windows. It took her a few minutes to settle in and close the door. Because of this, I was able to get a good look inside the car. I caught a glimpse of a man, but couldn't make out his face. Right before she closed her door, I saw something else. I squinted my eyes. It was none of my business, but it seemed a bit odd, especially considering the conversation we had. Then again, maybe it was my medicine, and I hadn't seen anything. If my eyes weren't playing tricks on me, then her father had just handed her a big envelope full of money.

Chapter 17

"Well, maybe it really was an envelope with money, and she's just lying to you," Saith said, biting into his pizza.

After Paris left we'd moved next door to the pizza shop. I let him call my mother and tell her everything was okay. She yelled at me first for hanging up on her, which I knew was going to happen, but Saith smoothed everything over. He told her his appointment ran over a little, and he'd gotten there thirty minutes late. He apologized, giving me an angry eye the whole time.

"I don't want to lie to your parents," he said, taking another bite. I noticed how his bites were larger than mine and he was almost done his first slice.

"You should've gotten a veggie pizza," I said. "Healthier."

"Well, you shouldn't be trying to set me up to be killed by parents, so it looks like we're even."

I stuck my tongue out at him. "Can I live?" I said, putting my pizza down and staring out the window.

"Bre," he said, lightly touching my chin and turning my face to him. "You can. And you are, but living doesn't mean reckless."

I took a swig of my water. "Every request I have, even the ones that follow their rules gets a 'no' or thirty questions. Cashmere and Desmond don't have to go through that."

He swallowed his pizza and swigged the last few drops of his soda. The waitress came over to refill his drink for him.

"You told me that Cashmere gets the third degree all the time and I'm pretty sure Desmond and your father butt heads a lot. They're too much alike not to," he said.

I frowned. "Whose side are you on?"

"The side that keeps you here as long as you can be," he said, grabbing my hand and kissing it lightly.

I smiled. "Don't flirt with me, I'm still upset that you're cutting our date short. We don't have much time."

He grabbed a napkin and wiped his mouth. "You can blame Paris for that. I said I'd have you home by six and that's what I'm going to do. In all fairness, that's three hours. My father is meeting us at the train station, so we should make it in time."

"You got the tickets, already?" I asked.

"Yep," he said, pulling them out of his pocket. "Train comes at five ten. We've got a good thirty minutes before we should start heading over there."

The train station was eight blocks away, but they weren't that long. That made me smile knowing we'd get to spend some time with each other. The cool spring air hit us as soon as we stepped outside. I loved Philly in the spring. I often dreamed of living in the country, where it was always nice and nature was beautiful. The big city lights and the loud horn from the cab driver always brought me back to reality whenever I was downtown, but the air was still crisp. I could at least thank God for that.

"So, how did you like our first date?" I asked Saith. I kissed his cheek, pushing him along as we walked through the after work crowd. Even in the midst of the hustle and bustle, I still felt like Saith and I were the only two there.

"This isn't our first date," he said.

I sucked my teeth. "Well, it's our first real one beyond the courtyard."

"And without your parents breathing down our necks," he said, grabbing my hand and slowing down. "You wanna go for a ride?"

I looked at him. "You mean on your lap?" He nodded. "The whole way to the train?" He nodded again. "I don't think that's a good idea."

He frowned. Then, a sneaky smile spread across his face. "Too bad you don't have a say in it."

He pulled me onto his lap before I could object. I squealed and laughed the whole time, urging him to keep going.

"We have to stop at red lights," he teased, as I wrapped my arms around his neck. I guess I could understand how Cashmere felt whenever she went on a date. If it was anything like this, I couldn't blame her for coming home late.

"Okay," Saith said, out of breath. "You've gotta walk the last two blocks." He grabbed his leg as I got up. "Whooo. That was fun."

I noticed the look on his face. "You okay?"

He brushed it off. "Yeah, yeah. Just tired."

As we neared the station and got on the elevator, I looked over at Saith. "Why did you grab your leg after I stood up?"

He shrugged. "It's no big deal. Just a slight pain."

"But you felt it," I said, my eyes lighting up. "Isn't that a good thing?"

"It comes and goes, I told you that. Temporary paralysis. I never know when my body is going to do what it wants."

I nodded. I got just as excited when he felt pain but found myself cringing in my own. He reached up and held my hand as we got off the elevator. Once the train arrived, we relaxed as I settled into my seat. I didn't realize how tired I was until I found myself sleeping on the ride home. It wasn't until we were in Mr. Richards' car that it hit me that I still had to talk to Mama. I looked over at Saith and reached for his hand again. He turned his head toward me and held my hand. He smiled. As we pulled into my driveway, I saw Mama waiting at the door. I was just grateful I'd gotten another kiss from Saith before I had to face her.

❀ ❀ ❀

"Next time, I'll make it my mission to accompany you if you can't follow my instructions, Bre," Mama said.

She'd been lecturing me for the last ten minutes about how important it was to keep in contact whenever I was out. And of course, she sliced into me for hanging up before she finished her statement. I listened without a word. It would only make things worse.

"Sorry, Mama," was all I said, but she still wasn't done.

"Bre, I'm just asking you to be careful," she said in a softer tone. "I love you, baby. You have to keep in touch at all times."

"How about I stay in forever, and we won't have to worry about anything? Maybe you can stop working on your business and homeschool me until I go off to college? Or maybe, we can all be homeschooled and that way, Desmond and Cashmere can take turns babysitting me? Wouldn't that make everything much easier?"

Mama took a deep breath and looked at me. "If that's what I needed to do to protect you and keep you safe, I would."

Our front door opened and slammed shut. Mama and I both froze. She quickly dabbed at the corner of her eyes and walked over and hugged me. "Love you, sweetie."

I wrapped my arms around her waist. "I love you more, Mama."

"I never said that Dad," Desmond said, as they both walked into the kitchen. "Mom, can you please tell Dad that I can work on other things and still take over the family business one day?"

Mama rolled her eyes in the air and made a gag face at me. I giggled. "Oh, boy. Double D trouble is here," I teased, walking over to hug Desmond. He hugged me back, but his eyes were still locked onto Papa. I could tell from the tension in his hug that they'd been arguing on the way home.

"I never said you couldn't," Papa said, kissing Mama and grabbing a water from the fridge. "It's just that you have to know how to build a business and when it's time to hand it over to someone in the next generation to delegate. That's how you focus on maintaining a family business."

"Enough, you two," Mama said. "Why are you even talking to Desmond about taking over when you're still alive and well?"

Papa looked at her and then back at Desmond. "I'm just letting him know the Clover system. Trying to groom him for it and he's missing the whole point. Nobody said to give up your dream; however, there is nothing wrong with having an empire."

Papa's cell phone rang saving Desmond by the bell. Judging by the look on Desmond's face, Papa may have been the one that was saved. I knew my brother's dream was to have his own business and empire outside of the Clover brand. It's what all of us wanted, yet it was different for him. Papa put more pressure on him because he was the only male. I looked at my brother and gave him a little smile.

"It's okay, baby," Mama said, kissing his forehead like he was a little kid. "Why don't you and Brelyn go and play some ball or something. Take your mind off of work."

Funny how Mama pushed him to relax and play but I had to get a permission slip just to walk to the end of the driveway. I had to say, Mama keeping a secret from Papa was a big deal. She was certainly showing some trust in me.

"Wait," Papa said, coming back into the kitchen. He'd stepped out to take his call. "We have a problem."

We all turned to face him. He walked over to Mama and me. "Dr. Warhol was in a car accident."

Mama gasped. I looked at Papa intently. "Is he going to be okay?"

Papa looked down at the floor. "It's bad, Bre. Really bad." He put his cell phone back on his waist clip. "That was his practice. They are sending over someone different starting next Friday."

Mama grimaced. "Who is he? Do we know him?"

Papa shook his head. "No. And I leave for Napa Valley in a week."

Papa's summer traveling was about to start. He always went away from the second or third week in June until the middle or end of August. He was back in time for us to start school. Most of his wine business took place in California, but his travels took him from the West Coast to West Africa. He spoke at wine conventions, went to different business conferences and numerous other events common to a wine connoisseur.

"Honey, you know everything will be fine," Mama said. "You still have a week. Bring a few doctors in. If we don't like them, we'll just go back to the hospital for weekend check-ups until we find someone Bre is comfortable with."

Papa turned to me. "Bre, are you okay with that?"

Great call, Papa, I thought. At least he asked. "I don't want to go to the hospital unless I *have* to. I'm sure if it was someone that Dr. Warhol's practice suggested, they're fine. You trust him, right Papa?"

He walked over to me and smiled. "Yes, baby girl. I do. Dr. Warhol and I have known each other for almost ten years now. I'm going to call his wife, then Mama and I will ask about this," he grabbed his phone and looked at the screen, "Dr. Michael Brandenburg."

"I heard of him," Desmond said, snapping his fingers. I'd almost forgotten he was still standing there. He'd been so quiet.

"How, son?" Papa asked, walking over to Desmond. "Is he any good?"

One thing about Papa and Desmond – they always got back on the same page when it came to the women in our family. Papa trusted him and his opinion - a lot.

"I've heard his name a lot," Desmond said, pulling out his phone. He hit a few buttons and scrolled down. "I can do some research."

Papa smiled. "Okay. Go ahead, son. I'll get on the phone with a few people."

Desmond walked over to me and showed me a picture on his phone. "Not a bad looking guy. He better not flirt with my baby sister."

I swung at him. "Shut up."

He was a nice looking man in his early forties. He seemed a little too young for all that his website claimed he accomplished. I shrugged it off, figuring it was all the more reason to trust him.

❀ ❀ ❀

It wasn't even a week later before my pain returned.

"It hurts," I said, trying not to scream again. I wasn't sure what brought about the attack, but it was shooting from my knee all the way up to my shoulder. Here I was in severe pain just two days before I was supposed to see Dr. Brandenburg and a few days before Papa was scheduled to leave. It didn't come while I was playing basketball with Desmond or doing anything else that my parents were afraid would give me aches and pains. I was lying in bed when it hit me. I screamed. The sharpness of the pain knocked the wind out of me. Desmond, who just happened to be coming in my room to tickle me out of my sleep, found me crying and grabbing my knee.

By the time we made it downstairs, I was writhing and crying, barely able to keep my eyes open.

"Shit," Papa cursed, throwing his cell phone down. "I leave Monday morning, and they just told me that Dr. Brandenburg is away in Spain conducting research."

Mama was rubbing my back and trying to open my pills at the same time. The prednisone was a low dosage, and in my current state, I felt like I needed the entire bottle. She grabbed a glass of water and Desmond held my head to his chest as brought the pills up to my mouth. "Here sis," he said.

I opened my mouth just enough for him to pop the pills inside and chug down some water. I rolled onto the bed and cried into the pillow. God, please take this pain away.

"Who are they sending now?" Mama asked, grabbing me and holding me. The mere sound of her heartbeat against my

177

eardrums used to be enough. Right now, it was just background noise to be drowned out by my loud screams. In between my sobs, I could hear Papa on the phone.

"Dr. Richard Lowes. Never heard of him..."

"Papa," I said. I knew where he was about to go. "Just get somebody here." I looked at him, panting. "It doesn't matter who it is. Please."

He looked at me. I stared into his eyes. There was that familiar look again. I forced a smile on my face. It took a lot, but I managed to reach out to him. He walked over and grabbed my hand. "It's just a test," I said. "Remember. It's just a test."

He nodded. "And we pass our test with our faith. It's the only way we can see what's on the other side."

I smiled as I wiped a tear from his eye. "You know how we do."

He gripped my hand. "I know you always used to encourage me with that when I was sick. We pass all the tests God gives us because He trusts us with the exam."

I nodded. "Please, just call him. Stop standing in God's way."

My faith was and always would be the anchor that kept me grounded. Times like this reassured me that regardless of how much money my family had, or how many people knew our names, life would always be filled with pain and heartache. The choice to rely on God was simple. He made it easier; even for a teenage girl like me who couldn't understand why I'd been chosen to bear this type of cross.

🍂 🍂 🍂

A few hours later I felt a bit better, especially now that Saith was by my side. "I'm just glad the medicine kicked in," I said to Saith. He was sitting next to my bed, working on one of his final papers. "The new doctor will be here tomorrow evening."

He stared at me. I looked at the mirror to the side of my bed and began fixing my hair. When I looked back over at him, he was still staring at me.

"What?" I said.

"Well, I have a few questions," he said. "How'd you get your parents to say 'yes' to me coming over without them sitting around or at least sending in a bodyguard?"

I laughed. "Papa doesn't like seeing me in pain. Not to mention, I usually can milk about a good week out of Mama after I have a major attack. She usually says 'yes' to pretty much anything I want."

"You're a bad girl," he teased. "I like it."

I smiled. "So, what're other questions?"

"You said God stepped in before the medicine did," he said. I closed my eyes quickly. I was cool with Saith having doubts about faith, but I refused to allow anyone to push their own doubts onto mine. I waited for him to finish. "What did you mean by that?"

"Well," I started, sitting up. "It's not anything magical. I just know I was praying from the moment my attack started. My mind felt the pain, but my heart was able to whisper prayer after prayer." I paused. "Between the Tylenol, Advil and the occasional dose of prednisone, I'm usually okay. This particular time Mama could only get the prednisone to me before the pain got out of control. Those little pills usually fill me back up with a shot of adrenaline but it takes a few hours. I stopped crying in twenty minutes."

"After taking it?" he asked.

I nodded. "Yep."

He turned back to his laptop and tapped away at the keys. "I'm reading this article about the young girl in Miracles from Heaven. You know the movie DeVon Franklin and TD Jakes did last year?"

I nodded, smiling. "Yeah. I loved that movie."

"I understand that miracles happen. I believe in them. I guess I just never associated it with something that was ongoing."

I propped my elbows up on my legs and rested my chin in my hand. "What do you mean?" I asked him.

"Well, I think when people think of miracles, they think of these big moments when God steps in, like how he did here," he said, pointing to the article. "But from what you experienced and from what you said, it's the little miracles that people don't think of that happen every day."

"Right," I said. "It's not always this big event. If I have a good day with no pain, that's a miracle to me. If I experience massive pain and take my medicine, but it kicks in immediately, that's even better."

He grinned. "I think that's cool that you believe that much. It's like, nothing can bring you down," he said.

We stared at each other for a few minutes. Then Saith made a silly face. I made one back. I reached out my hand, and he grabbed it. I threw my legs over the bed and stepped down. I sat in the recliner, which was right near where he'd stopped his chair. I made sure the room my parents set up for me didn't feel or look like a hospital room. Across from the two recliners was a love seat. It was like a small apartment in our home. There was even a little refrigerator by my bed.

"So, did you check to make sure there were no security breaches?" I asked Saith.

He looked at me. "Funny."

He was about to read over a few emails I'd received for business inquiries. We agreed that he could screen any incoming emails, especially on days that I was out of it and couldn't get much done. We set up an autoresponder email, but I think it made him feel special knowing I was allowing him to help me with something that was important to me. He was so protective, I started teasing him and calling him my personal security. Papa used bodyguards when he traveled, but he called them his armor bearers. They were just licensed armor bearers. Mama was just glad they never had to actually, "bear their armor" if you know what I mean.

"You got an email from a guy named Hank McDowell," Saith said, reading the email. "He says he knows your parents."

"Read it to me please," I said sweetly, batting my eyes. "I'm feeling a little weary and don't think I can keep my eyes open much longer, sir."

He reached over and tickled my neck. I grabbed his hand and kissed it. Smiling, he pulled his hand slowly away and put his attention back on the email.

"Dear Ms. Brelyn Clover, I'm not sure if you remember me, but your father and I go way back. I don't think I've seen you since you were five or six, but I heard about all the great things you're doing and wanted to see if maybe you could help me with weight loss. LOL. I'm about to launch a new business, and the doctor says my health isn't getting any better. You know your Pop and I used to run track together back in the day? Well, that young man is long gone. Gotta keep these organs well oiled. I met with a trainer last month, but our schedules are too conflicted. I've already reached out to your father to let him know I'd be contacting you. I know you have to be mindful of your health, but I assured him that I wanted to support your business venture instead of giving the money to someone I don't know. This is my personal email and phone number. Let me know how you wish to precede."

Saith laughed when he was done reading.

"What?" I asked.

"He may want to run spell check before he sends another email. He used "precede" instead of 'proceed.'"

I grabbed the laptop and rolled my eyes in the air, playfully hitting Saith. "Oh, give the poor man a break. He's my father's age."

He turned to me as I propped my feet up on the arm of his chair. "You remember him?"

"Not much. I remember my father telling me they had a business together years back. They split ways years ago, but I remember he came to an event my parents had right after one of my birthdays." I glanced at the email again. "I noticed he sent this last week before all of this started. If he contacted Papa first, I'm sure he told him that I could only email him a kit and nothing more."

"Maybe when your dad calls, you should make sure it's okay."

I looked at him. "Do you approve sir?"

He laughed. "As long as he's not some teen hunk, I'm cool with that," he said, winking.

Chapter 18

Dr. Lowes arrived the next morning promptly as scheduled. After brief introductions and some mild interrogation, he immediately began examining me. "Her vitals are as expected," the doctor said, giving me another dosage of medication. "I just want to make sure they stay that way. She shouldn't have had an attack that severe. We're going to try to increase her dosage of corticosteroid by giving it to her through the IV."

He moved around and inserted the needle into my IV. I winced a little. I could feel the medicine going through my veins. Other than being a bit cold, there was no pain at all. Mama and Papa stood there, glaring at him like they were hawks and he was an extra sack of mice.

"Desmond, come in here will you," Papa called out.

My brother came walking in. "What's up, Pop?"

"Okay Dr. Richard Lowes, here's the drill," Papa continued, turning Desmond and Mama so they all were standing in front of me. "That's our baby girl. I don't know you, but you came recommended. I expect you to treat my daughter better than you would your own. I'll be away on business, but believe me," he said, chuckling, "if something does go wrong, you're going to wish it was me and not my wife you have to deal with."

"Or me," Desmond said, giving the doctor a smug smile. "My father's right, though. Mama is a lot worse than any of us."

I watched as Mama gave the doctor a slight smile. I looked back up at him. I saw his Adam's apple move up and down. They got him, I thought. He'll be fine. I hated that Cashmere was out again, missing out on all the action. Then it dawned on me that she was probably getting more action wherever she was.

"Listen, I can assure you she'll be okay," Dr. Lowes said. "During my weekend visits, I'll check to make sure everything is going well and make sure she has the proper dosage of medicine. If anything changes during the week," he looked at Mama, "you have all my information."

He'd already given them his home, office, cell and his wife's number. Earlier, before he was allowed to come near me, I heard Mama grilling him. He'd pretty much handed over everything except his social security number. If Cashmere were here, we'd bet money that Mama would have that within forty-eight hours after he left. As Dr. Lowes packed up his things, Papa walked with him to the door. Desmond walked over to the side of my bed.

"I'm going to start dinner you two," she said, turning back to blow us a kiss. "Desmond, why don't you work down here for a bit?"

I bit my bottom lip to keep from saying something I would regret. Desmond rubbed my hand.

"Got it, Mama," he said.

When she left, he went over and closed the door. I looked at him. He gave me a weak smile. "At least they're letting you work with Hank, and I heard he's paying you more than what you quoted him."

"Yeah. Mama only approved because he called Papa first and got permission," I said, crossing my arms. I'd forgotten the IV was there and felt a pinch as soon as I did so. "Ouch."

"Careful, sis," Des said, rubbing my arm. "Anyway, you need to call your sister. She won't answer my phone calls."

"Cash?"

"Who else?" he said, irritated. "Emé has auditions this week in LA."

I grabbed my cell phone and scrolled through to see if I had any missed texts or calls from Cash. "She's probably doing her usual thing. She hasn't called or texted me since Wednesday. When was she last home?"

Desmond leaned down closer to me. "Wednesday. She's playing with fire. If Mama catches her ass before we can talk to her and at least *try* to cover, she's dead."

"I'm not sure that's a bad thing with the way Papa's splitting the will," I whispered.

He laughed, shaking his head. "You always know how to see the sun in the midst of a storm, don't ya?" He pulled my ponytail. "Proud of you for finishing this year strong. A 3.4 isn't easy. And don't beat yourself up because I know how you are. That's a good GPA."

"I know it is. Emé said the same thing you did; don't beat myself up."

"Let me grab my laptop, sis," he said. "You can work on whatever you need for Hank, and I'll do some designing down here. How's that?"

"Can I have a milkshake?"

185

He stared at me. He turned and looked at the door. "How you expect me to get a milkshake with the incredible hulk standing in the kitchen cooking?"

I pinched him. "Don't talk about my Mama." I reached out my hand bidding him to pass me my laptop. He gave it to me. "And the same way you used to sneak the weed you were smoking at one point. You figured it out."

I ducked as he grabbed a pillow off the couch and threw it at me. "I'll make sure to spit in your milkshake."

I stuck my tongue out at him as he left out, shutting the door. "Don't forget to add sugar to that," I yelled out.

As I settled in, my phone chimed. *Miss you. Hope you're feeling better. Maybe we can have a courtyard date this Sunday. Saith.*

I smiled. I scrolled through my emails with one hand and typed a reply with the other. I went back through my business emails, one by one. *How'd I missed this?* I opened an email from Paris that I must've gotten before Hank sent his. I hadn't heard from her since our face to face meeting, but then it dawned on me that it was June. *She must've gotten the money.*

Before I opened it, my phone rang. It was Cashmere.

"Cash, where the hell are you?" I said, without saying hello. "Two days? You must be looking to get buried at a young age."

I heard her pop her gum. "Relax kid," she said. "I called Emé, she's going to cover for me. I'm in L.A. with her now."

I almost bit my tongue. "What are you doing out there?"

"How I got out here is none of your business, but I called her before coming out. I just need a little vacation," she said. "No big deal. I'm about to call Mama now."

"So you called me to get your lie together, huh?" I asked. "If it were no big deal, you would've called Mama on Wednesday."

"For your information, I talked to her Wednesday night. Both our voices were at about a hundred decibels though, so I doubt we heard each other," she said. I noticed how sad she sounded. "Look, I just called to check on you. Des left me a message saying Dr. Warhol was down and out. I know you were comfortable with him."

I smiled. "Yeah," I said, sighing. "I just pray he's okay. They sent another doctor over, and he seems pretty cool."

She chuckled. "I'm sure he was after Mama's third degree and Papa' stare down."

"And you know it," I said. "I wish you were here. We could've giggled at how he squirmed in his pants."

There was a brief silence. "Look kid, I gotta go. I love you," she said. "Stay strong and take your meds."

I sat up in my bed a little. We'd been on the phone for at least ten minutes, and Cashmere hadn't asked me one question. "Are you sure you're okay, Cash?"

"I'm good. I promise," she said. I thought I heard a sniffle. "Let me call Mama."

"Okay. I love you, too."

She'd already hung up. I was praying Emé would talk some sense into her. It was hard to get Emé's attention when she was working, but if she let Cashmere come out there now, she had a plan to do something. I felt a tear drop on my hand. I quickly wiped it away, knowing Desmond would walk in again at any moment. Just as I put my laptop back on my lap, he came in holding two cookies-n-cream milkshakes.

"I told you I loved you," he said, kissing my forehead and putting my shake on the table next to me. He had his laptop tucked under his arm.

I guzzled it down like it was my last one. "How'd you get past S.W.A.T.?"

"Dinners brewing. She's in her office working. Perfect timing."

I winked. Desmond put his headphones in and started working. I turned my attention back to my laptop. I opened the email from Paris.

Hi Brelyn,

I know it's been awhile, but I'm happy to announce that I'm able to do a more in-depth plan at this time. I wasn't sure at first if I would be able to, but luckily for me, the summer job pays well, and my dad loaned me the money until I get my first pay. Let me know how to precede with paying for the one-month kit you recommended. I know you offered to allow me to do it in two payments instead of one. Looking forward to your reply,

Paris

I smiled. A milkshake and two clients all in one day. I couldn't be happier.

❦ ❦ ❦

The rest of the day passed quickly, and Dr. Lowes's next visit came in no time.

"How's that?" Dr. Lowes asked me.

"Good," I said, happy to have the IV removed from my arm. We'd agreed that things seem to be getting back to normal and I could try a few days without injections.

"You feeling better?" Mama asked. Nodding, I smiled. She'd been more relaxed these days. I'm guessing between preparing for the launch of her new line and all the other things going on, she was able to balance between overwhelming me every five seconds and getting her work done.

"I can sit with her for a while," Cashmere said, walking in with her laptop.

Mama gave her the longest stare I'd ever seen. Without saying anything, she walked over to me and kissed my cheek. "Love you, baby," she said. She turned to Cashmere. "Call me if she needs anything."

Cashmere pursed her lips. "I'm sure I'm capable of grabbing her water and ice chips."

The sound of her tone made me turn to Dr. Lowes and see if he was paying attention. I think he was trying not to, but there was no way he couldn't feel the amount of heated estrogen in the room. My heart was beating fast. Mama had no shame in discipline, and I was betting that Cashmere would have a bed right next to me. When Mama left the room, I looked at my sister.

"You know you're pushing it, right?"

She winked. "Just giving her what she expects. Why let her down?"

Before I could respond, Dr. Lowes turned back to me. "I think we're good for today. Once I do my visit tomorrow evening, I'll be able to better assess how your body responded to the steroid injections. Otherwise," he said, putting his pen in his shirt pocket, "you're doing great, kiddo. Keep it up."

As he closed his laptop and grabbed his briefcase, I noticed his screensaver was a picture of a girl.

"Is that your daughter?" I asked.

He snapped his head in my direction. "Oh. Oh. The computer?" he stuttered. "No. My niece."

Cashmere gave him a weird look and looked back at me. She put her finger near her ear and made a circular motion. I tried not to laugh. "Why is he acting so weird?" she whispered to me.

"Well, Cash," I said, "you do have that effect on men."

She stuck her tongue out at me and walked back over to the couch. Plopping down, she snapped open her laptop.

"I'll see you tomorrow," Dr. Lowes said, waving goodbye before tripping over the rug in the room. "Take care now."

He barely looked at Cashmere when he left. I glared at her. It didn't help that her shorts were up her behind and her tank top was ripped so that the line in her cleavage was more visible than the crack of a plumber's behind when he bent over. Only Cash didn't have to do anything for her breast to show. They just did.

"You're sickening you know that?" I said to her. "When'd you get in?"

"Last night. Late."

"Red-eye?"

"I caught a flight after we spoke. Mama made me. So, here I am," she said, never taking her eyes off the screen of her computer. "Cool Cash is cashing in."

I sat up. I looked at the clock on my bedside table. It was almost three, the time Saith and I had set for our FaceTime meeting. He was going to help me with some business things, and I couldn't wait. It reminded me a little of how my parents worked together when Papa was away. Mama would check an email or two whenever he asked her, and she'd respond on his behalf, depending on the nature of the email. I knew Saith and I were nowhere near my parents, but I felt a little more responsible having someone I liked be in my corner the way Papa was in Mama's.

"Saith and I are about to have a business meeting," I said to my sister. "Can you give me like thirty minutes and come back?"

She raised her eyebrow at me. "A business meeting, huh?" She stood up. "Business meeting my behind. If you want to talk to your boo in private just say that."

"Maybe you can bring back some popcorn and lemonade when you come? Then we can watch a movie on Netflix or something."

She smiled. "Sounds good. You need anything else before I go? Is your water pitcher full?"

I chuckled. Just when I thought my sister wasn't being herself, she'd come back in full swing.

"Nope," I said, opening my laptop. "That's it."

As soon as she closed the door, I called Saith. When his face came up on the screen, I smiled. "Hey you," I said.

"What up?" he said. "How you feeling?"

"Great. I actually think Dr. Lowes is better than Dr. Warhol," I said. "Not that Dr. Warhol did anything wrong, but I haven't been as tired lately."

He nodded and stuffed something into his mouth. "Good stuff."

"What you eating?"

"A bagel." He smiled. "With low-fat cream cheese."

"You suck," I said, laughing. "You can eat whatever you want. Don't say I didn't tell you so."

"Says the girl who had a milkshake the other day."

"Yeah, yeah, yeah," I said. "So, what's next. Did you see the email from Paris?"

"No. I only check it when you need me to. Other than Hank's, I haven't seen any."

Made sense. I only *needed* Saith to step in when Mama kept the laptop from me for hours on end. I had Cashmere and Papa to thank for that. Between his upcoming departure and her disappearing act, I'd been able to focus without many interruptions.

"Well, she got the money," I said, pulling up her email. "It looks like her summer job is going well and she can do the plan that I recommended."

He clapped. "Good stuff, my lady." He turned his attention to someone else. "Myla, Dad said you couldn't go without me. I'll be ready in a second."

I stopped smiling. Saith didn't tell me he was going somewhere. I thought we were going to talk for a while.

"Sorry about that," he said. "We can't talk long, but I still have a good ten minutes," he said. "You need me to do anything before I head out?"

I sighed. "No, uh, not really. I just wanted to talk to you."

Somewhere along the way, I'd gotten used to our two-hour conversations. The small ones in between were a tease. He sat back in his chair.

"You know," he said. "I love your hair like that. You keeping it?"

"Maybe," I said. "Got it done early this morning."

Mama had our stylist come by, and I chose to get two strand twists. The summer was here, and I didn't want to battle with my hair. More importantly, I had no idea how the medication would affect my hair, so I opted for something more manageable.

"Don't give me a compliment to take away from the fact that you're cutting our date short," I said, crossing my arms.

"I'm not cutting it short," he said. "We never agreed on a time. You just said three."

"You're right," I said. "Okay. Well, since there were no other business emails, I guess that's it."

He laughed. "You girls are something else." He pulled a shirt over his head and started getting dressed. "You and Myla act just alike sometimes."

I frowned. "What is that supposed to mean?"

"Whenever someone doesn't move on your time or do things immediately, you give them an attitude and start to pout," he continued. "And you're both good at that reverse psychology thing. Making guys feel bad."

"Well then," I said, shrugging. "I guess it doesn't matter if I do this."

I ended the call. I knew I was being petty, but he made the wrong move comparing me to another girl. I guess that was something he hadn't figured out about women. Just as I was about to get up and go to the bathroom, I heard my parents passing my room. It sounded like they were arguing. I tiptoed over to the door.

"I just think you should wait until July," I heard Mama say. "She's doing better now, but this doctor is new. Even with everything checking out about him, my business launch is coming up."

I heard what sounded like a zipper. I knew that Papa was putting his suitcases by the door.

"Sherese," I heard him say, "you do this every time I leave, whether your business is having a launch or not. I know about Brelyn's health which is why I pushed everything back a week."

I didn't hear Mama respond, but I knew she was probably standing there with her arms crossed, poised, waiting for Papa to give in. It worked with us most of the time. A King can't do much without his Queen on a chess board, but I'd learned as a kid that our chess board was unique.

"We have a private plane," Papa continued. "I'll be on the first thing back if something happens. And I'll call Brelyn every day."

"What about your other daughter?"

"Our daughter is going through what most teen girls go through," he said. "Rebellion. When I gripped her up last year, you insisted I was being too hard on her. You said you would handle it. In fact, you begged me to let you handle it."

"So it's my fault Cashmere is acting out?"

"No. It's nobody's fault but hers."

I heard their feet shuffling around. I backed up a few steps, praying that neither of them was coming in. I was thankful the floor was carpeted. Holding my breath, I tried peeking through the crack of the door. I could see Papa moving around and Mama standing beside his large suitcase. I noticed there were two bags. He was definitely going to be gone for at least a month. I knew the large one held a few suits, slacks and buttons up while the other one probably had all his casual clothes he'd wear when he was running around having fun.

"Is Bill driving you to the airport?" Mama asked.

Papa stood in front of her. He walked over and grabbed her in a tight hug. She stood still for a minute, then slowly wrapped her arms back around him.

"You know I love you and will do anything to see you smile," he said. "But one thing you and Cashmere have in common is that stubbornness."

"It's why you've been with me for almost twenty years," Mama said. "And it's also why I needed you to bring me balance."

Their foreheads touched, and they kissed. I closed my eyes for the minute that I knew they'd be sucking on each other's faces. I know it's how I got here, but I still didn't want to see it. When I opened them again, Papa was walking toward the room. I slid across the carpet quickly, bumping my leg on the edge of the hospital bed. I ended up on my behind just as Papa opened the door.

"Bre," he said, rushing over to help me up. Mama was right on his heels.

"Baby, what happened?" she asked.

I don't want them to argue again. I had to think quick.

I started laughing. Hard. I laughed until tears came out of my eyes. "I'm fine. I fell being nosy. I was staring at Carlos, the pool guy," I said, helping myself up and pushing them away gently. "See?"

When we all walked toward the window that faced the back of the house, Carlos was indeed doing some form of the Macarena with his headphones on. He was sweating and working hard, but the dancing was just unbearable. My wit kicked in quickly, remembering Mama made most of the appointments and calls from my room. I'd waved at Carlos just a few hours before. Thanks, Carlos.

"But, how did you fall?" Papa asked, laughing himself.

"He caught me watching. I was rushing back to my bed," I said. "Ow." I rubbed my knee. "I was actually on my way to the bathroom. You all set to go, Papa?"

"Yes," he said.

I walked over to the bathroom and shut the door. I waited a few minutes, then flushed the toilet. Taking a deep breath, I headed back out. What I saw when I came out brought a smile to my face. My parents were hugging. Again.

"Quit it, you two," Cashmere said, walking back in. She had the popcorn and a pitcher of lemonade. She also had Oreo cookies; my favorite.

"Hey, sissy," I said, winking at her. "Thanks."

Mama looked at me. "The popcorn is okay, but the lemonade and Oreos may be a bit much."

I looked down at the napkin. "I'll only have a few cookies."

"Well between that and the milkshake you had the other day, I would think that would be enough."

Busted. "How'd you know?"

Papa laughed. "She's Mama. She knows everything."

He walked over to me and grabbed me in an embrace. "Do you want me to stay a little longer, Bre? I will if you need me to."

"Nope," I said, popping an Oreo in my mouth. "I'll be fine, Papa. I'm fine now. I think the shots helped me a lot. Other than bumping my knee on that rail, I'm good."

"And we're all here," Cashmere said. "She'll be fine. I'm going to hang around the house and help out more this summer."

Mama raised an eyebrow. "Are you?"

Cashmere looked at her. She turned to Papa. "Yes, I am. Cool Cash has been doing pretty good."

"What are your quarterly sales so far?" Papa asked her.

"Thirty-two hundred dollars, after the maintenance fees and other stuff," she said.

Papa high fived her. He grabbed her in a soft headlock. "Proud of you. Now, if you can just stay focused on the business and stop messing around with these broke suckers, I can keep your Mama out of jail this summer."

Mama grunted. "Or her for that matter."

"Babe," Papa said.

Mama threw her hands up. "I'm just saying."

Cashmere walked over to Mama and opened her arms for a hug. "Well, I won't be in jail this summer, because my Mama raised me right. Isn't that right, Mama?"

I watched as Mama wrapped Cashmere in a hug. "That's right, big head. You know I love you."

I breathed a sigh of relief. I wasn't ready to deal with them fighting, especially while Papa would be away. Desmond could only calm Mama down so much. As they hugged, I caught a glimpse of Cashmere's face. I'd heard her words clearly, but she could never hide her facial expressions. She's up to something. I could tell by the sneaky grin on her face.

Chapter 19

The next few weeks went smoothly, especially with my health.

"Thanks, Dr. Lowes. See you next week," I said.

He gave me a little wave and a smile as he left. It's been three weeks since he started and things were going better than ever. I was feeling like the old Brelyn again, but with a brighter focus. Whatever steroid he was giving me was helping. I didn't mention to him that there was some pain yesterday. I figured that was just the norm for me – to expect pain sometimes and to smile when it didn't happen. That was easier said than done, but there was no point in making a big deal about one bad day when I had six others to be thankful for.

"Somebody's got a crush on their new doctor."

I smiled as Saith rolled into the room. "What makes you say that?"

"Well, considering I hadn't come in yet and you have this silly grin on your face, I'd have to say it was him that put it there."

He stopped next to the bed and reached for my hand, giving it a little squeeze.

"Nope," I said. "I was grinning because I remembered that we had a date."

"Glad that I'm not in the dog house any longer," he joked. "I'll set my laptop up over here. I've been working on some things myself."

He placed his stuff on the small desk Mama had put in the other day. It kept me from being confined to the bed.

"You haven't been in the dog house in three weeks. You were the busy one," I said. "What are you working on?"

I pulled out my laptop and waited for it to turn on.

"Remember I told you that I used to make up stories for Myla when she was younger?" he asked. "Well, I decided to turn them into a series." He made his way back over to me. He tapped away on his keys, then turned the screen towards me as he approached. "Introducing the Sugar and Spice series."

I looked at the screen in awe. There was a picture of a girl and a boy. On one side, the boy was in the dirt and was covered in mud. His head was turned to the girl, and he had his tongue sticking out. There was a frog by his foot and a bug in his hand. On the other half of the picture, there was a girl with flowers in her hand, from the same garden the boy was standing in. She was super clean and had on a pretty yellow dress. The sun was on both sides of the picture.

"Wow. Is this the cover?"

He nodded. "Boys are snakes and snails and puppy dog tails," he said. "That's what I used to tell Myla. I decided to do a newer version of the old adage my mother said her grandparents said to her all the time. So when I would make the stories up, it was always about a boy who did something crazy and a girl who was irritated by it."

I scrolled down to see more. "Kind of like you and me," I teased.

He kissed the top of my head. "But I'm not this dirty, and you're not that clean."

I swatted at him, but he got away with just one quick spin of his wheels. He moved faster in his chair than people did on foot.

"I love it. Did you draw that yourself?"

"I sketched it. Had one of my friends draw it out so I could really capture the essence of the story."

"How many stories do you have?"

I reached for my water and drank everything that was in the glass. The dryness in my mouth came out of nowhere.

"Thirsty?" he teased. "So to answer your question, I have about six stories to start."

I beamed. "That's amazing. Look at that. The athlete has a softer side."

"I've learned that I've gotta have something more than basketball," he said. "Even without an injury, there has to be more that I can build on."

His tone got lower when he said that.

"Hey," I said. "This is only temporary. Remember that. No matter what you do, don't let go of your dream."

If only I were that sure of my own destiny.

✿ ✿ ✿

Some time after I fell asleep on Thursday night I woke up and rushed to the bathroom. I made it just in time to the toilet before everything that I'd eaten today came up. I wasn't sure what was going on, but this was my routine since Monday afternoon. I felt chills running up my spine. A kind of chill I'd never experienced before. It reminded me of the winter the Philadelphia area had gotten six years ago – thirty inches of snow surrounded everything. Shoveling with my siblings was fun until my toes and fingers grew numb. The vomiting wouldn't have bothered me so much if the tingling sensation in my hands and feet wasn't so irritating. I had no idea what was happening, but Dr. Lowes assured us everything was okay.

I crawled back to my bed, grabbing the edge of it. With my sheets in my hand, I attempted to pull myself up. Breathing heavy, I managed to rise up on my knees. God, please. Where is this pain coming from? I thought. Just yesterday, there was only throbbing in my knee and some pain in my stomach. Today, my body was definitely turning against me in a way that I'd never thought it would.

Sweat dripping from my face, I looked over at the clock. 2:00 a.m. I was glad it was Friday. Dr. Lowes would be here later today. When I felt the next shot of pain go up my spine, I knew I couldn't wait that long. By the time I was back in the bed, the clock read 2:15 a.m. I looked at the pager button Dr. Warhol had set up when he first started. Until now, I'd never used it. I knew it would ring out to Mama's room, but I couldn't deal with her right now.

I reached for my phone and put in my code. I hit the one button. I could barely hold the phone to my ear. I put it on my chest and waited.

"Sup, sis? You want another milkshake?"

I'd never been so happy to hear Desmond's voice.

"Des," I managed to say. My voice was just above a whisper. "I need you."

I closed my eyes.

God, I know you told us that there would be battles we don't understand. I know I shouldn't even question you. But I have to ask 'why'? Do all babies in the family suffer like this? Was I meant to bring my family together with my suffering? It's the one thing that keeps them together, I know. This can't be your plan. I have so much life to live. I want to see the world. I just had my first kiss.

"Bre," Desmond called out, busting into the room.

My eyes fluttered open. "Des," I said, a tear streaming down my face. "It hurts."

My mouth could only utter those few words, but I was still praying in my heart, hoping God was listening.

God, please don't let this be it. I want to go to college. I want to make my parents proud. And I want to know that I left something with my name behind.

"What hurts, Bre? Tell me," Des said. He was sweating as he lifted me up and jumped on the bed behind me. He let my body rest against his. "Come on, baby sis. What's wrong?"

I turned my head just as more vomit came out. Desmond didn't even move. He just yelled for Mama.

"Mom! Mom!"

I saw him reach for his phone just as my body felt like it couldn't hold on any longer.

Now I lay me down to sleep. I pray the Lord my soul to keep. If I should die before I wake. I pray the Lord, my soul to take.

I used to hate that prayer when I was younger. I always felt like a child should never have to pray that prayer to God.

God, I don't want to die. My heart started beating faster. *Please. I can't imagine my Mama standing over me crying.*

The last thing I saw before I blacked out completely was Mama and Cashmere running into the room.

Have your way, Lord. Thy will be done.

Chapter 20

"It was probably just too much of the steroid," Dr. Lowes said. "I'm going to lay off of it for a week or so to see what happens. To be clear, she still needs to take the Tylenol and Advil for her milder pain."

I took a deep breath and slowly removed the oxygen mask from my face.

"Will I be okay?" I asked him.

Mama was rubbing my forehead and keeping my head cool with a cold rag. Dr. Lowes looked at me and forced a smile. "Just stay focused on being healthy. I'll take care of the rest."

Desmond stood up just as Dr. Lowes was nearing the bed. "That answer doesn't suit me too well," he said.

"Desmond," Mama said, stepping in. Desmond glared at her but kept his mouth shut. "It doesn't sit well with me either. You have some explaining to do besides telling her to stay healthy. She's been doing that. Why did her body react the way it did?"

Mama's voice was getting louder. I knew it would only be a matter of seconds before Dr. Lowes saw a different side of her. I reached up and gently squeezed her hand.

"Mama," I said weakly. "It's not his fault."

"Brelyn, stop. Nobody is saying that. You just relax." She turned her attention back to Dr. Lowes. "My question has nothing to do with whose fault it is. I know it isn't his. I'm asking what happened."

He looked at her. "Her body had an adverse reaction to the amount of prednisone that I gave her." He put his hand up as Mama opened her mouth to speak again. "I gave it to her in a low dosage the first weekend. As Brelyn discussed feeling discomfort and pain in her knees, I increased the dosage, little by little. When she had a good week, I didn't do anything because there was no need. However, if you recall last weekend, she said she was dizzy, and she could barely move her right arm."

Mama nodded. "I remember. She said it was hurting more than normal."

"Yes. So I gave her a little more. Her body could be reacting to the combination of the steroid injection with the prednisone dosage."

Mama's chest was heaving up and down. She was calming down. A little. "So what do we do now?"

"Monitor her," he said, walking over to the monitor that checked my heart rate. "She hasn't had lupus a year yet. There will be times her body reacts differently to different medications until we know which ones are best. It's just a part of the process."

I used my free hand to move my bed up to a comfortable position. Dr. Lowes came over and put the oxygen tube in my nose and removed the mask so I could move around easier. "How do you feel now?" he asked, checking my pulse.

"Better," I said. "It's not as bad as it was earlier this morning. I still feel nauseous, though."

"She hasn't been able to keep anything down since late Monday," Cashmere said. "Is there something we can do as far as that? What about tubal feedings? Isn't a week without food bad?"

For once, nobody looked at her like she was crazy for asking twenty-one questions. I was sure we were all wondering the same thing. What does all of this mean *now*?

Desmond picked up his phone. "It's Papa."

"I must've missed his call," Mama said, turning to look for her phone. "Put it on speaker, Desmond."

When I heard Papa's booming voice through the phone, I grinned. "Papa," I said, as loud as I could.

"Hey, baby girl," he said. Desmond walked closer so Papa could hear me. "How's my angel?"

"Not good, Papa," I admitted, with tears streaming down my face. "Not so good."

There was silence. It had been a long time since I'd admitted to not doing well. Most of the time I could deny it because I was denying the disease. There was no denying it now. Lupus had walked right up to me and slapped me where it hurt most - my pride.

"I'll be home by Sunday evening or early Monday morning. I talked to Emé, and she asked the set director for a few days. She should be there by Wednesday or Thursday at the latest."

I started shaking my head. "No. She texted me earlier and said the same thing. I won't allow it."

"Bre, stop," my brother said, with tears in his eyes. "You talk like you're some servant of ours that we aren't supposed to care for. You're not a burden."

I turned my head away from him. I'd shared that with him during one of our private conversations after I'd first been diagnosed. When I turned back to him, a tear was dropping from his eye.

"Listen, your brother is right," Papa said. "Stop taking this so lightly. You need your family around you now, and that's where we're going to be. It may not be all at the same time, but we're coming." He choked up. "Just promise me you'll fight."

Whatever tears I'd been fighting to keep from falling were now freely flowing. Cashmere was lying in bed next to me with her head resting on mine. She was holding my right hand. Mama was holding my left hand, and Desmond was standing next to Mama. If they weren't trying to scare me, they had a funny way of showing it.

"Okay," I said. I mustered up some strength to say what I needed to say. "I'll do it on two conditions."

"Anything," he and Mama said together. She smiled.

"One, that you guys stop sitting around this bed like you're saying goodbye to me. This is not hospice care, and you guys are creeping me out."

Papa laughed. "I can actually see it without even being there."

"You'd be right on her other side," Desmond said, teasing. "Right in front."

After we shared a laugh, Papa spoke again.

"What's the other condition, baby?"

I swallowed. "That Saith gets to be here, too."

Mama stopped smiling for a second. She looked at Cashmere. Desmond shrugged.

"He's not bad, Mama," Desmond said. "I actually have to say that he's almost as decent as me. Almost."

Papa cleared his throat. "If it makes her happy, that's fine."
I smiled. "But Bre?"

"Yes, Papa."

"If anything goes wrong while he's there, I'm going to blame him."

All I could do was laugh. At least there was some sense of normalcy, even if only for a minute. As another pain shot up my leg, I could at least be thankful for that much.

***

When I woke up from my nap, Saith was sitting over on the couch sleep. Desmond had helped him get onto it, which didn't seem as hard for him as we all thought it would be.

"You guys think I'm some cripple," he had joked. "I have to sit on a toilet sometimes too, ya know?"

Even Mama laughed at his joke. Now, as I stared at him, I realized why it mattered to me so much that he was there. I smiled more when he was around. My heart also sped up a bit. It wasn't the same feeling I got when an attack came on. My heart would beat faster in a good way – just like when Papa used to come home with everybody's favorite ice cream. I could see him at the end of our old driveway as a kid. My heart would speed up the closer he got. And right when the ice cream was in my hand, my heart would return to normal. Saith starting moving around. When he opened his eyes, he looked around. When our eyes locked, my heartbeat slowed down again.

"Hey, pretty girl," he said, wiping at his mouth. "You feeling okay?"

"Come closer," I said, reaching my hand out to him. "You need me to call Desmond?"

"No," he said, sharply. "I got it."

He slid his body closer to the end of the couch where his chair was. He moved the chair around, so it was facing him. I watched as he hoisted himself up by the handles and sat down.

After taking a few deep breaths, he moved the foot adjustments down and settled into the chair.

"You comfortable?" I asked him.

He nodded and turned to face me. "I have something to show you." He placed his laptop on his lap and rolled over to me. "You remember that email you received from Hank?"

I sat up. "Yeah. What about it?"

"Did he contact you again and purchase a plan?"

I shifted my way to face him better. "Yes. I sent it to him last week. Why?"

"I took a look at the emails like you asked me to do. You know, the two days you were completely out of commission?"

"Yeah. I remember. What's up?"

"Well, I noticed something strange," he said. He tapped away on his laptop, then turned it and handed it to me. "Look at the two emails. The last one you got from Paris and the one from Hank. I put them side by side so you can compare them?"

I read over the emails twice. I didn't see it at first. When I read each one again and got to the end, I saw it. I gasped. They both used *precede* where it should've said *proceed*. It was at the end of the email, and the last sentence was even similar. *Please let me know how you would like to precede.* I hadn't checked my emails since Monday night. Between the vomiting and fatigue, I just couldn't bring myself to do it. So I asked Saith to keep an eye on the business stuff this week.

"Wait a minute," I said. "That's just too much of a coincidence."

"Same thing I said," he said.

I looked at him. "What made you even go back and read these?"

"Well, you told me to check and at least respond to emails when you were down, so people wouldn't think you were dropping the ball with your business. When you got another email from Paris, she said something that rubbed me the wrong way."

"What was it?"

He pointed. "Go to the email she sent yesterday."

I scrolled through and opened it.

Brelyn,

Hey. Thanks again for sending over that plan. I just wanted to check in to let you know things are going well. I've been sticking to it, but it can be hard when traveling. I took your advice on preparing meals early and packing them, but how do I stick to my plan when I'm on the go?

Write back when you can,

Paris

"Okay," I said. "Maybe I'm missing something. There's nothing crazy here."

"You're right," he said. "However something about on the go just kept bothering me. You and your parents said that Dr. Brandenburg was traveling for research."

"Yeah and that his practice referred Dr. Richard Lowes."

"That's the thing," Saith said, moving closer to me. "When I googled Richard Lowes, a lot of different people came up. None of them were doctors."

My heart was beating faster again. "Wait. None?"

He shook his head. "None. Something is off."

I reached for my cell phone. "Did you call the practice to see?"

He shrugged. "I thought your family had already done that."

I grabbed my head. I was starting to feel dizzy again. *That doesn't make sense. Desmond said he checked.* If there wasn't a Dr. Richard Lowes anywhere on the internet, then surely something was wrong.

"Desmond said he would look him up, but I guess he forgot once he got here. Things were going so well before this week." I said. I could feel my stomach churning. This man had been in our home for almost a month now and possibly wasn't a doctor? "Maybe the internet is off."

Saith frowned. "Bre. It's Google."

I nodded. As I attempted to text Desmond, my hands started shaking. The phone fell onto the floor.

"Bre, what's wrong?"

I couldn't answer him. My body immediately started convulsing. *Oh my God. It's happening again.* I'd only had one seizure since being diagnosed. As I struggled to breathe, I tried to grab onto the bed, but my hands were hitting the side of the rail. I saw Saith roll to the door.

"Help!"

Mama ran in and reached for the monitor. "It's okay. It's okay." She didn't touch me. She just waited until my body was done.

"You okay?" she said, as tears left my eyes. "It's okay. It's okay. Just breathe. Just breathe."

I was so disoriented by the time the rest of the family came in. I stayed quiet as everyone crowded around me.

"It was just a small seizure. You're fine," Mama said. She looked at Cashmere and Desmond. "She's fine."

I held onto her waist with all the strength I could muster. I looked over at Saith. He wasn't moving. I knew he was scared. Desmond followed my eyes. When he looked at him, he smiled.

"Hey, she's fine. Bre's a fighter, you know that," he said. "Come over here. She needs all of us."

Desmond walked over and pushed Saith closer to me. I could see the fear in his eyes. Although my arms were still around Mama's waist, he reached up to rub them. I smiled weakly, happy he was there. Only this time, the fluttering in my stomach wasn't.

❦ ❦ ❦

Papa arrived home as soon as he could, and of course, I had to share the news Saith discovered about Dr. Lowes. To say that he was not pleased with Desmond was an understatement.

"I did look him up," Desmond yelled.

Papa looked at Desmond. He'd just landed a few hours ago. Since he'd been home, he and Mama were arguing about whose decision it was to bring in Dr. Robert Lowes. Cashmere laid on the bed next to me with Emé was on speaker phone.

"Wait, wait," she said. "Guys. Let's just focus for a minute, okay? Wait," she paused. "Yes. That's fine. Whatever flight will get me to Philadelphia International Airport the quickest is the one I need. Yes. Okay. That's fine ma'am. Coach is fine."

I looked at the phone and swallowed. Nothing was scarier at that moment than hearing Emé fly coach. If she was taking whatever flight she could and not waiting for a first class seat, that led me to believe things were worse than I was hoping. Why else would she rush to get here? I knew Mama called her. I didn't want them all standing around my bed. It was too morbid.

"Okay, I'm back," she continued after a minute. "Listen. We all make mistakes. Now is not the time to point the finger."

"That's funny coming from you," Cash said. Papa gave her a death stare. She continued playing with my hair. "Sorry, sis. Go ahead," she said.

"I'm not sure who this guy is. None of us are. The important thing is to figure it out. I'm just wondering why Dr. Warhol's practice would refer him if he isn't a doctor."

"I was thinking the same thing," Papa said.

"Does anyone know his status? Is he still in a coma?" Emé continued.

Everyone looked at each other. Silence.

"We've all been so concerned about Bre," Mama said. "Between the businesses and the travel, no..."

She started crying. Papa walked over and held her. "Stop. This is nobody's fault." He turned to Desmond. "Not even yours." He pulled him into their embrace.

I smiled and squeezed Cashmere's hand.

"Mama, why don't you call Dr. Warhol's wife and check on everything. Maybe she can tell us more about this Dr. Lowes. I mean I'm sure after thirty something years of marriage, she knows who he trusts, and she should know what doctors are in his immediate circle."

"Didn't you guys say the recommendation came from Dr. Brandenburgs's office?" Cashmere asked. "Wouldn't that mean you'd have to speak to him?"

Papa turned to Desmond. "Son. Do you remember?"

"Dr. Warhol's office recommended Dr. Brandenburg," Desmond said. He grew quiet.

"What? What is it Desmond?"

He shook his head and sat down. With his head in his hands, he prayed. "God, I don't know what is going on, but I know you do. Please fix this. Give us the answers." When he stood back up, he walked over to me. "I'm sorry."

I grabbed his hand. I looked back and forth between him and Cashmere. Emé's voice came through the phone.

"Desmond, what is it?"

His eyes welled up with tears. Papa walked over to him and grabbed his shoulder lightly. "Son, we're a family. We all make mistakes. It's okay."

Desmond looked back at me and wiped his eyes. "I was the one that let him in. It's all coming back. It was Friday evening. There was no answer at Dr. Brandenburg's office, but I left a message giving him Mama's cell phone. When Dr. Lowes showed up, I assumed they'd gotten the message."

"Mama, you talked to him that night, right?" Cashmere asked. "Didn't everyone say he was okay? You guys said Brelyn liked him?"

"Yes, Cashmere. Any doubts we all had were erased by Brelyn's improvement. She felt better the first few weeks he was here. She sounded better, she..."

Mama was speaking so quickly, she was sputtering.

"Mama, it's okay," I said. "She's right. Whoever this man is, he made me comfortable. I didn't start to experience any discomfort until last week."

Papa looked at me. "Okay, so today's Tuesday. When was the last time he was here?"

"Sunday afternoon. He came early because he said he had another appointment."

"Desmond, do you remember anything about him? Anything at all."

"When he showed up that day, he had everything a doctor would have. He showed me his ID, he had a doctor's bag just like Dr. Warhol would carry. He looked and talked like a doctor."

"It's okay, son. I wouldn't leave until I knew for sure Brelyn was comfortable. He knew that."

Papa turned and slammed his hand against the wall. Desmond moved in his direction, but Mama raised her hand to stop him. After a few deep breaths, he walked back over to us.

"He fooled us, all of us. Nobody missed their steps. We didn't do anything wrong, this son of a gun purposely made us believe that everything would be fine. That's why Bre's body didn't start acting up until the last week. He played all of us. He made sure we would trust him. He took his time just like a snake would."

Cashmere sat up. "It makes sense. Nobody would think to double or even triple check if this guy came in talking like a doctor and looking like a doctor. If Brelyn didn't complain, everything was okay in her eyes." She rubbed my back. "And ours too."

Mama crossed her arms. "He even had an answer for why her body was reacting negatively and lowered her dosage of prednisone. And Brelyn slept okay that night. She wasn't one hundred percent, but she wasn't screaming like she had been the night before."

"If it looks like a duck, walks like a duck and talks like a duck—" Cashmere said, shrugging.

"But smells like a rat," Desmond interrupted her, "then it's a doctor walking around with a death wish."

He balled his fists up. Papa grabbed the back of his neck.

"Son, the one thing we have on him is that he doesn't know that we know yet. And even if he does, I'm already on it."

"Pop," Emé said. "What if he does know? Let's focus on figuring out what's wrong with Brelyn. At this point, we could be chasing the wind. He'll get his in due time. We have no clue

214

what he's been giving Brelyn, and that should be our primary focus."

My heart started speeding up. I hadn't even thought about the fact that if this guy is a fraud, he could've been trying to make me sick on purpose. But why?

"Why would someone do this to me, Mama?" I asked. I hadn't meant for it to come out, but I'm sure I wasn't the only one thinking it.

She walked over to me. Cashmere got up so Mama could sit down. She grabbed my head and held it against her chest. "Baby, I don't know. I just know that everything is going to be okay."

As she wiped another tear from her eye, I rested my head against her shoulder. "How do you know?"

She sighed. Her answer surprised even me. "Because you've taught me that it will."

"I'm just asking that you let us work this out until we know what's going on. Can you just trust me, Bre?"

My body may have felt weak, but when Papa said Saith couldn't come over today, I felt a surge of adrenaline. We'd been going back and forth about it for the past twenty minutes.

"I don't get it. Just last week he was the golden boy, now he's the prodigal son again?"

I knew I was being disrespectful. I'd already asked Saith over before my parents came down to check on me. Now, I had to call and cancel.

"Well," I said, crossing my arms and pouting. "You can send him away when he gets here. I already invited him over."

"Brelyn," Mama said.

"Nobody told me things had changed."

My parents both looked at me. I was right. They should've told me that they were back in "trust nobody mode" before I called him. Mama walked over.

"I tell you what," she said, looking at Papa. He gave her a nod. "Why don't I cook your favorite and let Saith come over

for dinner? How's that? And you can tell him to come later."
She started fluffing my pillows. "Huh? How's that?"

I rolled my eyes. "A compromise. Sounds like a plan.
Except he has a therapy session today. Not sure when he's
going to be done. How do you know his family doesn't have
plans for dinner?"

I felt a pain jolt up my arm. I uncrossed them but didn't
say anything. I was still puking everywhere, and nothing could
be held down. They'd been making calls all day to make sure
things were in place at the hospital. Ever since we'd realized
something wasn't right with Dr. Lowes, Papa and Desmond
made calls to determine who he was. Emé would be here soon.
Desmond and Cashmere waited on me hand and foot.
Everything was right and returned to our recent version of
normal; except Saith wasn't here and Dr. Lowes hadn't been
answering the number he gave us.

"Honey, Dr. Warhol's wife is coming over later," Papa
said. "I invited her for dinner."

He looked at me. A sharp pain shot up my back. I couldn't
hide this one. I grabbed my back and shut my eyes.

"What is it, honey?" Papa asked, flying to my other side.

"My back. It feels, it feels—" I couldn't finish. The pain
was increasing with every word I spoke. Mama grabbed my
hand and helped me lay down. I looked up at the ceiling. I
blinked back tears and grabbed the side of the rail.

"Desmond, she needs to go now. We can't wait another
day for the hospital," Mama said to Papa. "Now."

"Baby, I'm just making sure everything is okay before we
get there. I don't want this to happen again. How do we
know—"

"We don't," Mama said sternly. She glared at him
intensely. I could see Papa fidgeting with his phone. "And

we've been able to see that no matter what you do or what security system we have, the only thing protecting our baby is God."

"I get that," he said. "Let me just make a few more calls."

Mama walked back over to Papa and snatched his phone out of his hand. Cashmere and Desmond walked in at that point. A few seconds later, Emé pushed into the room.

"My baby will not die because of your ego. We're going to the hospital."

Everyone stood frozen in place. I blinked several times. I was crying uncontrollably. I reached up and wiped my face with what little strength was left. I sniffled. Emé came rushing over to me as Mama and Papa continued staring at each other. Mama's chest was heaving up and down. Papa looked at me. Then back at her.

"Hey, sis," Emé said. "You okay?"

I nodded as she hugged me. She looked back at Mama and Papa, then at me again. She looked at Cashmere and Desmond. They walked over and we all locked hands. Desmond held out his hand, waiting for Mama to walk over. She didn't move. Papa grabbed her hand and pulled her. She started moving her feet. When Papa clasped hands with Cashmere, Mama looked around at all of us. She reached out and grabbed Desmond's hand. I smiled.

"No more fighting," I said in a low tone. "Please."

"Papa, we're going to the hospital, okay?" Emé said to him. He closed his eyes and nodded. A lone tear fell out of his eye."

"Okay," he said. "I hear you. Let's do it. Is that okay with you, Bre?"

I winked at him. "Yes."

He nodded, and Mama nudged him.

"You're the man of the house," she said. "You pray."

He took a few deep breaths, then he looked up at the ceiling. "God, we need you. We need you bad."

Everyone closed their eyes except me. I looked at each of my family members and realized the scene wasn't as morbid as I thought it would be. The sight of my family surrounding me actually made me believe that if this were the end, I wouldn't want to go out any other way.

When we arrived at the hospital, the nurse took us right up to the room Papa asked them to prepare for me. When I saw it, I laughed. When Papa demanded the finest, he got it.

"I see you pulled out the big guns, Papa," Cashmere said, pushing into the room. "I bet you Blue Ivy couldn't top this."

Everyone laughed. I was glad the tension had left, at least for now.

"Yeah, Papa," I said. Desmond helped me out of the wheelchair and into the bed. I looked at the nurse. Poor girl didn't even have a chance.

"I'll be back to set up her IV and everything once you guys get settled," she said.

"Thanks," I said, smiling at her. She gave me a little wave as she left the room.

Once I was in my bed, I adjusted myself. Everyone started moving around, asking me what I needed and what they could do to make it better. Did I want this plant here or there? Did I want the table closer, where I could reach my laptop or was it okay here? Did I want something to eat now or in a few hours?

"How about everyone just relax and stop making me feel like I'm talking to four Cashmere's," I finally said.

Cashmere looked at me. "Ha Ha."

Once everyone started to relax and quiet down, I spoke again. "I just want to feel like I'm at home. Having you all here is enough. Until the new doctor comes in, I just want to rest."

Mama nodded. "And that's what we'll let you do." She started rounding everyone together. Emé sat down in one of the chairs. "Cashmere and Desmond, you guys don't have to stay here. I can have Papa take you back home, and he can come back."

They both shook their heads at the same time. "No. We're not going until we know what's going on."

They locked hands. Mama's nostrils flared.

"Mama, it's okay. Nobody has to leave," I said. "I just want peace. Relax."

I patted a spot on my bed and moved over. She slowly walked over and sat down. I kissed her cheek. The nurse walked back into the room.

"All set?"

"Yes," I said. "Let me change into a gown."

I grabbed my purse and headed to the bathroom. Once inside, I started undressing. I grabbed my cell phone out of my bag and called Saith. He picked up on the third ring.

"You there?"

"Yes. I'll let you know what time to come by tomorrow. It'll probably be best to come Thursday afternoon. By then, I should be feeling a little better."

"Okay. You know you can beat this, right?"

Tears sprang to my eyes. I wasn't so sure. "Yes. I know. How was your session?"

"Great," he said, yawning. "I'm just tired."

I finished putting on my gown with my free hand. I switched the phone to my other ear. I could hear my family talking to the nurse. I knew Mama would be knocking in a few seconds.

"I gotta go. I'll text you tomorrow," I said.

"Okay," he said. "Wait."

"What's up?"

"I love you."

Smiling, I mustered up the courage to say what I'd been writing in my journal for the last week. "I love you, too."

❀❀❀

By the time Dr. Warhol's wife arrived, Dr. Snyder, who was my regular pediatrician, had already run multiple tests. When Mrs. Warhol walked in, I didn't want to see another person at that point. My body was throbbing, and the pain in my knee felt like it had dried in cement. Dr. Snyder couldn't give me anything other than morphine for pain. He had to figure out what was in my system before he could pump it with more medicine. I wiped some of the sweat from my forehead. Mama rushed over with the cool rag she had been using.

"Don't," I said, stopping her. I was tired of being babied.

"Hi, Brelyn," Mrs. Warhol said. She walked over and gently touched my hand.

I forced a smile on my face for her. "How's Dr. Warhol?"

"He's out of the coma, but he's still out of it." She sat down and looked at Mama. "I was so ready for those lovely crab cakes you make."

Everyone smiled. Even me. Mrs. Warhol looked at me again. Something was off about her. It was like she had something to say, but she was afraid. I pushed the button to raise my bed. I looked at Desmond, and he walked over.

"What is it, Bre? You need the doctor?"

I looked at Mrs. Warhol. "What's wrong? Were you able to ask Dr. Warhol anything about Dr. Lowes?"

I could tell Desmond picked up on my vibe when he softly squeezed my shoulder. He turned his attention to Mrs. Warhol.

"Anything you can tell us would help, even the smallest thing."

She looked down and opened her purse. "Well, my husband wasn't able to tell me much because his mouth is slightly twisted from the accident. We mainly communicate by writing notes to each other." She paused. "He used to write me love letters in college all the time."

She reached into her purse and pulled out a piece of paper. "When I asked him about Dr. Richard Lowes and told him what you guys think may have happened, he wrote this."

Mama and Papa both went to grab the piece of paper from her, but Papa got it first. He opened it up. He looked at Mama, then at me. Emé stood up.

"What? What does it say?"

Cashmere walked over and snatched the paper from Papa's hand. She came around to Desmond's side and showed him. I was irritated that nobody felt the need to share it with me. From the look on Desmond's face, I realized it may have been something I didn't need to know. But, when I looked back at Mama and Papa faces, my curiosity got the best of me. And when Emé slapped her hand against the wall in anger, I snatched the paper from Desmond's hand.

"Bre..."

My heart started beating faster as I read the big, black words on the page. I felt the tears sting to my eyes, and through the blur, I could read the words: *NOT A DOCTOR ANYMORE.*

Everyone was loudly talking over each other at this point. Even the two police officers in the room couldn't keep them quiet. Three hours passed since we'd all discovered the truth about Dr. Richard Lowes. His medical license was currently suspended by the State of Pennsylvania. Two years ago, a family filed a malpractice lawsuit against him for overdosing their four-year-old son. Apparently, his alcohol addiction got the best of him, and he would come into work late, reeking of liquor. Patients would literally leave their appointments when he came out to greet them. His private practice had been shut down immediately upon the investigation, but there were a faithful few.

"I understand how you feel," Officer Gray said. "I do. Mr. Clover, you and I have known each other for years, so you know I'm a man of my word. We'll take care of this, but you've got to trust us and calm down."

Papa walked over to him. He pointed at me. "There is nothing on God's green Earth that will keep me from making sure that low-life gets everything he deserves. That's my baby. Mine!"

He was shaking. Mama went over and touched his shoulders. "Dear, it's okay. Trust me, we're on the same page. I have your back, but you have to calm down."

His eyes were still fixated on Officer Gray. He shifted his eyes toward me, and I swallowed. I gave him a slight nod. I knew he was fighting for me, but I needed him to stay level headed.

"Papa, it's okay. We'll figure it out," I said, holding out my hand.

He let out a deep breath and walked over to me, grabbing my hand. He hugged me and kissed the top of my head. "I'm so sorry I wasn't there to protect you."

I caught Emé's eye. She walked over and rubbed his back. "Papa. You were there. It's okay."

I knew that was hard for her to do since they still hadn't worked out their issue, but one thing that always brought a smile to my face was my family's ability to put it all aside for what really mattered – family.

"So, where do we go from here?" Desmond asked. "Have you arrested him yet?"

One of the other officers spoke up. "Uh, well, we're just trying to locate him." He looked at Officer Gray. "Has your doctor told you exactly what's wrong?"

Desmond frowned. "What do you mean, what's wrong? I'm not understanding."

We all looked back and forth at each other. Then it hit me. "You mean you need evidence before you go and arrest him? Why does that matter if he shouldn't have been there in the first place?"

Cashmere looked at me, then back at the officers. "Yeah," she said. "I mean I get needing evidence but doesn't the fact remain he shouldn't have shown up at the door. He's not allowed to practice medicine."

"Even if he was, he did something to my daughter, and I know it," Mama said. "She was fine..."

"Mrs. Clover, you said that Brelyn was experiencing pain off and on. Lupus does have those effects. I do not deny that he was wrong, and he will be arrested, but until her doctor comes back with solid proof, I'm just going to lay out the truth here."

He turned to Officer Gray. He looked at the other officer who hadn't spoken a word since coming into the room. The silence that was piercing the room must've been too much for Emé.

"What? What the hell is it?" she blurted out.

"He's still under investigation, and his license is suspended, but there's a piece missing. Something is way off about this situation. How did he know about your daughter's sickness? You said Dr. Warhol didn't refer him, but he knows he's no longer a doctor, right? Okay, well what does he have against you for him to go through all this trouble?"

"Are you saying someone else is involved?"

Officer Gray walked closer to Papa. "They have to be. This makes no sense to any of us. So far, all of his patients that have still been seeing him are people he knows personally. People dumb enough or broke enough to seek him for treatment. Either they know what's going on and don't care because he's giving them a bargain discount on treatment or their loyalty is misguided. Either way, his connection to your daughter makes no sense to us." He looked around the room. "And apparently, it makes no sense to any of you either."

Cashmere started crying. Desmond walked over and put his arm around her. "What does that have to do with his arrest? Bring him in for questioning."

"We have issued a warrant, and officers have already been to his house. We're tracking him down the best way we can, with what evidence we have."

Emé crossed her arms and looked at him. "Please explain to me how this man even gets his hands on medication if his license is suspended."

"His private practice was in his home. Perhaps when they raided his home and shut him down, something was left behind."

Just then, Dr. Snyder walked into the room. He had a clipboard in his hand and a disturbed look on his face. He nodded at the police officers and walked over to me. Mama and Papa immediately turned their attention to him. He put his hand lightly on my shoulder.

"You feeling okay, kiddo?"

"As best as I can, considering," I said, glancing at Dr. Snyder. "What's going on?"

He sighed and grabbed the chair. "Can everyone just take a seat? Wherever you can. Please."

As he sat down and opened his clipboard, he looked at my Mama and Papa again. "I need you to let me finish explaining what's going on before you react. Just know, that Brelyn is going to be fine."

The way he swallowed after his statement told me he wasn't so sure about that. I squared my shoulders back and prepared for the worse.

"Your test results came back," he started, looking down, then back up at me. "Benlysta is a new medication that the FDA approved a few years ago for patients with lupus. It can be given either as a tablet or through an injection. And it most cases, the medicine works. There are side effects that are disturbing, but most lupus medications have side effects, and of course we know it depends on the person as each body reacts differently."

So far, he had my full attention. "If it's supposed to work, then why was I getting worse?"

He looked around the room and slowly stood up. He reached for my hand. "Brelyn, the medicine hasn't been proven to work in African-Americans."

Chapter 22

To know you've been given a drug that you didn't need was one thing. To know that the drug could literally kill you was something else. There were times where I'd felt so close to death, that I cried out to God to end it. Whatever the fake doctor had been trying to achieve had almost worked. Almost. I had so much to tell Saith, but I'd only been able to text him this morning. I'd have to fill him in later.

"So what do we do after you flush her system?" Papa said, breaking me out of my thoughts. I could tell from the weakness in his voice that he had very little fight left in him. He just wanted me to get better at this point. As the nurse and Dr. Snyder made me comfortable, he reached for my IV and inserted the needle. I winced.

"It's just the saline for the IV," he said, talking me through it. "Brelyn, I need for us to work together. I've known you since you were a little girl and I know we have a tight bond," he said crossing his two fingers.

I smiled and did the same. "Just like this."

He looked me in my eyes. "You can overcome this, but I need you to adhere to everything I say," he continued. "No more being stubborn about the process and overwhelming yourself with your business."

That one hit my heart, but my pain was overriding my passion at this point. Completely overriding it. I just wanted to live.

"I got it, whatever I need to do."

"We," Des said, looking at me. "We."

I nodded. "Well, since you're being so generous, can we switch bodies?"

As everyone shared a laugh, Papa walked over to me. "I actually wouldn't mind doing that right now," he said. "But you're the soldier, always have been."

I smiled and slowly turned my head to Mama. "It's fine. Mama, really. Dr. Snyder and I have it all under control."

She gave me her best smile. "And God."

"And God," I repeated.

When Dr. Snyder was finished cleaning my IV, he sat down. "Kimberly, can you call Laura in, please?" he asked his nurse. When she left the room, I reached my hand up to touch my Clover chain. I saw Desmond playing with his, too. Smiling, I turned my attention back to Dr. Snyder.

"Go for it, doc."

"Laura is one of the nation's top nutritionists. She's going to be here with Brelyn for the next month," he said. My shoulders dropped when I heard month, but I quickly shook off whatever doubts I had. My summer would be gone, but I'd rather spend the rest of my summer in the hospital getting better than a day at the morgue. "She's already put together a smoothie cleanse that will help detox your body. The best solution for us right now, after I flush her system the best I can, is to let her body take its natural course. I've done more research on Benlysta, and discovered that while many cases have failed in cases where it was used to treat African Americans, there were others where it did exactly what it was supposed to do. My guess Brelyn is that because you were keeping up with your regular medications and because there were steroids in your system, whatever Dr. Lowes was doing was hurting you, but helping you at the same time."

"So the guy really is an idiot?" Desmond said.

Dr. Snyder nodded. "A good one. Either he changed his mind when he was trying to hurt Brelyn, or he wasn't giving her the exact dosage that would've killed her. Whatever it was or whatever he was thinking, I thank God he was thinking it because it's the main reason why we can reverse this thing and get her back on track."

"I wonder why he did it," I said out loud. "Like if his point was to hurt me and he changed his mind, why not just stop coming? Why come for almost six weeks if you weren't going to carry your plan through?"

Dr. Snyder sighed. "Brelyn, when someone is crazy enough to try something like this with a very well-respected and wealthy family, my bet is to say he thought he could get away with it. Perhaps it kicked in that whatever he was trying to do just wasn't making any sense," he said. He looked at my parents. "Hell, Brelyn, I'm an actual doctor and the way your parents have breathed down my back for the last fifteen years gets me a little nervous. I'm pretty sure Mrs. Clover made him twitch more than once."

I laughed at his joke. "You are right about that. I think when he was leaving one day, I saw a tear coming out of his eye."

Dr. Snyder winked at me. "With that being said, my concern and focus are not him. It's you."

"He's going to pay for what he did," Emé said.

"And that's for the cops to handle," Dr. Snyder said. "My concern is Brelyn and nursing her back to health."

Dr. Snyder was right. The only thing that mattered now was me getting better. When Papa and Desmond didn't say anything about finding and killing the man, I knew then their focus was on the same thing. At least for now. I could bet money that Desmond's thoughts were sounding a lot like, *"Papa just taught me to shoot last year. That man better be lucky I don't have my gun license."* I giggled at the thought.

"So I basically can't have any more milkshakes or Oreos for the next thirty days?" I joked. "A whole month?"

Dr. Snyder smiled. "Two. The first month is just the detox and cleanse. The second month will be getting your body adjusted to a new regimen that will help you maintain your health. The most important thing with lupus is eating right and exercising."

I smiled.

"Light exercising," Dr. Snyder corrected. "Sorry to burst your bubble, kiddo. I'll let you know when you can go back to your fitness classes."

"I'm cool with it," I said half-heartedly.

Emé walked over and sat next to me, hugging me close. "It's just temporary."

I had a déjà vu moment from when Cashmere had said that to me just months ago. I thought about responding in the same way, but this time, I had peace about the outcome and whatever else was going to happen.

"I know."

🍂🍂🍂

After Laura came by, things were looking a little brighter. Everyone was more relaxed, and I felt a little stronger. Emé offered to order food for everyone while we waited, Desmond recommended that everyone have a smoothie so I wouldn't be tempted. Of course, Cashmere had to have a moment because her heart had already been set on ordering a cheesesteak and fries. But she gave in – with the condition that she could immediately order a cheesesteak when I went to sleep. To everyone else, Cashmere was being a brat. Papa had to quiet her and Mama down a few times. But I understood how she felt. Imagine having your norm ripped away just because of something you couldn't control? I felt compassion knowing that she was trying to support me the best she could. Had I not snuck and read that journal entry she'd left open on her computer that one time she stayed the night at Robbie's without anyone noticing, I wouldn't know that she'd been feeling left out since I'd been diagnosed.

"Have lots of ketchup and extra cheese for me, sis," I said. She gave me a thumbs up.

Desmond was on his laptop looking up information on Dr. Lowes. When he started showing everyone the stories he found, it was crazy. All we needed was more time. Had we had it, he would've never been able to step foot inside the house.

"I guess I'm still trying to figure out who would go this far just to prove a point and what point were they trying to make?" Cashmere asked.

"I think I can help you with that," I heard a voice behind Papa say. I felt my smile getting bigger as the recognition settled in. My stomach fluttered.

"Saith," I said. He rolled over to me and gave me a hug. His father was with him. For a minute, the pain was completely gone, and I'd even forgotten my family was there. That was until Papa cleared his throat.

"How you doing young man?" Papa asked him, shaking his hand. This forced Saith to have to let me go. He turned to his father. "Luke." They shook hands.

"Sorry about everything," Luke said. "Brelyn, I pray that they catch this guy. Saith told me what was going on."

Papa looked at Saith, then at me. "I didn't know they'd been talking much."

I knew his trust level had gone back down. I didn't take it personally at this point.

"Papa, Saith and I talk all the time," I said quietly. "He's my friend."

From the way he was clenching his jaw together, I could tell Papa had more to say. When he didn't speak, Mama stepped in.

"Thanks for coming by Saith. I'm sure Brelyn needs all the love she can get right now," she said. "Luke, have a seat right here."

Desmond passed a chair over to him. He sat down, looking at Saith the entire time.

"Son, why don't you tell them what you know," he said.

Everyone in the room, including me, looked at Saith. He took a deep breath, then reached into his backpack and pulled out his laptop.

"Bre, remember when you started having me check your messages to keep up with the business," he started.

"Bre," Papa said sternly.

"Desmond, stop it. Just listen for once," Mama said. Papa stared at Mama but didn't say anything else. Saith had her full attention. She grabbed my hand. "What can you tell us that can help my baby?"

He took a deep breath. "So, Brelyn asked me to check messages for her. In the beginning, I would just periodically look, like when she asked me to. But when all of this started happening and she started texting me that something wasn't right with her body, I thought about the time we met the girl Paris downtown."

I felt Mama squeeze my hand. I knew everything Saith said after this was incriminating. I also knew he loved me and wanted to protect me. I glanced at Papa. He looked like he was ready to pop. Saith turned his laptop to face me.

"Bre, you remember when you said you saw her get in a car with someone and you swore you saw a black man handing her an envelope full of money?"

"Yeah. I thought it was odd because she told me her father was picking her up."

"And Paris isn't black, I'm assuming?" Desmond asked.

"She's Indian," Saith said, "and she told Brelyn she was a sixteen-year-old girl who lives in Atlanta, Georgia—"

"Bre, how did you meet this girl?" Desmond asked me.

"Online," I said. "It is an online business," I said sarcastically. I knew everyone was thinking about how dangerous it was. "Paris emailed me after she sent me a message on Twitter."

Mama raised her hand to quiet everyone. "Go ahead, Saith."

"Well, I never trusted her, and I told Brelyn that," he said. "It wasn't because they met online. There was just something off."

"Bad vibes," Emé said. "Always go with the vibe." She smiled at Saith. "Good boy."

"Well, from the emails I wasn't sure, but when Bre and I were downtown together that Saturday and I'd finally met her, I couldn't shake the feeling."

"He could barely sleep that night. He kept saying he didn't feel right about the girl," Luke chimed in. Papa gave him a crazy look. "And for the record, I had no idea that it was supposed to be a secret and Brelyn wasn't supposed to be running her business. I knew she had been helping Saith with a few exercises and they liked each other. That's it."

"He's right, Papa," I said. "Before we had our dinner, the only thing we'd asked him was to keep quiet about was the training. He had no idea you guys told me no to both. He just thought I was being careful with my health and that you were smothering me."

"And did you give him that idea, Bre?" Papa asked.

I sighed. "Maybe."

"Anyway," Saith said, looking at Mama. "I decided to look her up. Like those guys do on Catfish. I put the image in the computer and tried to search it." He clicked on a few keys. "I came up with this."

I stared at the laptop and grabbed my stomach. My first smoothie of the day was on its way back up. "Malina Patel. Nineteen-years-old. Lives in Atlanta, Georgia." I looked at the picture. "That's definitely her."

Everyone tried to crowd around the laptop.

"Well, that was dumb," I said. "If she didn't want to be figured out, why use your real picture?"

"I think she underestimated your intelligence," Saith continued while Emé scrolled on his computer. "And your business skills. Your emails were always short and professional. I don't think she was bidding on having to work to do what she was doing."

Everyone looked up at him. "Which is?"

234

Saith took another deep breath. "I googled Malina Patel," he said, grabbing the laptop again. He typed in a few things. "And this is what I found."

When he turned it back to all of us, we gasped. We sounded like a chorus – all on one accord. I wasn't sure if Papa had even seen it.

"Papa. Isn't that — isn't that...." I could barely get it out.

"Hank McDowell."

Chapter 23

If only I had been more careful, things wouldn't have gotten this far. I know I can't blame myself, but Hank and Paris? How is this even possible? Did I ignore the warning signs? My parents will probably never trust me again.

Thoughts of confusion swirled my mind as I slept. I wasn't sure what part of today had been more exhausting – the four hours of testing or the two hours of questioning. The police arrived shortly after Saith revealed the photo with Hank and Paris, who we now knew was Malina Patel, a nineteen-year-old immigrant from India. That's all her website told us about her background. From the looks of it, she was some kind of photographer. Her website was full of photos. The one with her and Hank had obviously been taken by someone else.

Today's events were only the beginning of what I was sure would be an ongoing investigation. Mentally, I just didn't care anymore. If I wasn't fighting for my life, I was fighting to stay sane in a rich kid's world where everyone wanted to know your name because it would benefit them. If they were real friends, you barely got to see them because of restrictions either put in place by parents or life. The times you were able to be close, you had just enough time to share memories and some great food before you were called to do the next thing.

Like Desmond. Just this morning he and Papa were fine. But whatever had them butting heads for the last two months had been brought up here at the hospital. Papa's concern for me and safety was the perfect angle for him to use on Desmond. I knew my brother wanted to explore his options outside the family business. I knew he wanted to try something new. But I could've sworn I heard him say something about not going to college and I knew Papa wasn't having it. I was hurt that he hadn't told me that, considering we shared everything. I tossed and turned for another hour before I eventually reached for my phone. *Maybe he's still up.*

I started to type out a text but changed my mind. I dialed his number instead.

"Can't sleep?" he asked as soon as he picked up. It was like he was waiting for me to call him. Either that or both of us were mind boggled and trying to digest it all.

"Not at all," I said, sitting up. The light from the hall came through the crack in my room door. I didn't feel like getting up to close it. I just prayed the nurse wouldn't come in if she heard me on the phone. Since all had been revealed, Papa's reigns only got tighter.

"Me either," he said. "I was thinking about you, thought you were asleep."

"I was going to ask why didn't you just call."

"That's why I answered before you asked."

Smiling, I leaned back against my pillows. I hadn't asked him yet, but I had to know. I wouldn't be the girl who just assumed.

"Saith, what is going on between us? I mean, like what do you call what we have?"

He let out a deep breath. "I care about you. A lot. I mean, we went from giving each other ice grills to holding hands in your courtyard."

I chuckled. "Yes, we did. But you gave me the ice grill first. I was as sweet as pie."

"Are we talking about the same person here? The one who basically called me a punk for letting my condition get the best of me? Sweet as pie?"

"It worked," I said. "What did your therapist say?"

"She told me to be patient with the process. My body will figure itself out eventually." He paused. "For now, I'm grateful for the twitches of pain that I can feel."

"Funny how life works, right? One minute you ask God to take the pain away and the next minute you're grateful for the pain because you know you're alive."

"You have no idea how many times that thought has run through my head, and all I keep saying is 'wow.' To meet someone like you during one of the roughest times in my life was unexpected."

We both were silent for a second. I was hoping I wouldn't scare him with wanting to know what we had, but I like my father taught me, if he can't be upfront, then put him behind you.

"Why don't you come by tomorrow after your session?"

"I'm already ten steps ahead of you," he said. "To officially answer your question, I'd rather talk about it face to face."

I was grinning so much, I was glad he was on the phone and not here. "Call me before you come, okay?"

"Got it, Bre," he said. "Get some rest."

As I ended the call, I opened up my Instagram app. It was amazing what one could feel when looking at other people's pictures. The emotions ranged from sad, to disgusted to happy to inspired. It was the perfect symbolism for how I'd been feeling lately; sad, disgusted, happy and inspired. I was praying that the latter one would increase more so I could hold onto some light. As I continued scrolling, something caught my eye. *No way. There's no way.*

❀ ❀ ❀

"So she was at your launch party?" Officer Gray asked me.

"Yes. That's her right there," I said, pointing at Paris in the photo.

Last night, I thought I was high on the morphine Dr. Snyder had given me, but no amount of drugs could convince me I was wrong. Malina Patel had been in my home before she'd messaged me on Twitter. One of my father's colleagues had tagged her in the picture. The police already summoned her to the police station, but Mama was livid. Her coming to our home and then pulling something like this was unfathomable – it made absolutely no sense to put a target on your back. I looked around at my family, who once again had found a way to push everything aside for me. It seemed when we thought things couldn't get any more interesting, life was ready with another surprise.

"Okay, take us through the details," Papa said to Officer Gray. "What happened when you picked up Hank last night?"

"You mean three nights ago?" he said.

"Wait, wait," Papa said, holding his hands up. "You picked him up three nights ago, and I'm just hearing about this?"

Officer Gray shrugged. "Listen, I told you I'd contact you when we had details. A picture on a website doesn't make this guy guilty of anything, *and* both of these people were someone you guys knew to some extent. We needed him to crack."

Papa's nostrils flared, and he opened his mouth to say something but stopped.

"What happened?" Cashmere asked. "Did you pick her up too?"

Officer Gray raised his hand. "Everyone settle down, and I can tell you what we have," he said. "I'll start with you." He pointed at Papa. "Tell us about the business you started with Hank twenty years ago."

Papa's eyes grew wide. "What? What the hell does that have to do with anything?"

"Apparently everything or I wouldn't have asked you, Mr. Clover."

"Can you just tell us what's going on without the sarcasm and BS?" Emé said, stepping closer to my father. "Just in case you forgot, privileged people deserve respect, too."

"Emé, it's cool," Desmond said, touching her arm.

She snatched it away. "No, it's not. This prick has been acting snooty with us since day one."

Officer Gray relaxed. "Listen, I'm on your side here. I have to ask the questions. You guys seem like a pretty close-knit family. I'm sure everything I'm asking is something you already know. Right?"

She glared at him but didn't say anything else.

"I'm curious also," I said. "What does that have to do with what happened?"

"It's okay," Papa said. "It's okay. I'll answer."

We all looked at Papa.

"Before I completely took over the winery, Hank and I had a restaurant together," he said.

"The one you invested in?" Mama asked.

He nodded. "Hank was the chef. I was the investor. He came up with the business plan and everything. I didn't want to be involved too much, but I believed in him and his vision." Papa walked over to the window. He turned back to face us. "A year in, all the money was gone, and I told Hank I had to move on. There was nothing left to salvage of the business, but he insisted we keep going. I had a choice. I could focus on the family winery or continue to go into debt trying to help a friend."

"So you chose the winery?" Desmond asked.

"Yes. I did," Papa said. "It's the reason why I want you to start to learn the family business. It's safe."

He and Desmond stared at each other. Papa shifted his glance back to Officer Gray. "Hank was angry. Very angry. We didn't talk for almost nine years."

"That's why his email said he hadn't seen me since I was five or six."

Papa nodded. "Right before Thanksgiving, he called me out the blue, and we met up. It was like old times. Two friends, hanging out and having a beer. Only he had an agenda."

"Don't they all," Cashmere said.

"Yeah, they do, baby girl," he said to her. "He pulled a business plan out of his jacket pocket and wanted to discuss it, but I shut it down. We exchanged some words, but nothing substantial. People get upset. When we parted ways, I was under the impression he understood and that we were good."

"What gave you that impression?" Officer Gray asked.

"He said he'd call me sometime the following week and we'd get together again if he didn't have to work."

"And did you?"

"He called. We chatted, but we didn't hang out."

"So you brushed him off?"

Papa looked at him. "If you're asking me did one of us cancel, yes. It was him that said he had business to take care of, so he was flying out sooner than he thought."

"Officer, what is going on?" Mama asked, impatiently.

"Apparently, Hank never got over the first bad business deal—"

"It wasn't bad. It failed because he didn't understand business. He had the talent," Papa snapped.

"All I'm telling you is his side," Officer Gray said, flipping through his notepad. "For your information, Hank McDowell has been involved in numerous money scams, bad business deals and even some theft since you guys last talked. Apparently, he never got back on his feet since the first business deal went down. Malina. Dr. Lowes. It was all a part of his plan."

"Plan?" Desmond asked.

Officer Gray nodded. "Hank paid a receptionist at Dr. Brandenburg's office to let her know when the Clovers called and set up an appointment. Somehow, the call got routed to Dr. Lowes, who he's been in cahoots with for five years."

"So Dr. Lowes is connected to Hank and Malina?" Mama asked, sitting down. Papa rubbed her back.

"Yep. Apparently, Hank is not only good at holding grudges, but he's also good at convincing people he can help them with their situations. Malina needed to become a citizen, and Dr. Lowes can't practice medicine legally. Two people who had nothing to lose, but something to gain."

"Wait, wait," I said, slowly putting the pieces together. "That photo on her website was their wedding picture?"

Officer Gray nodded. "Quick marriage and she's a permanent citizen of the United States. All that mess she told you about her family being here is a lie. Now, Atlanta was true, that's where they met. But the rest of it, all a lie."

I shook my head. A sharp pain shot up my arm, causing me to grab it. Mama stood up.

"Bre?" she said. "You need the nurse?"

"No, no. I'm fine," I said. "Officer, were you able to get all the emails you needed from my hard drive?"

"Yes, but we needed to see the Twitter exchanges, too. All of it is evidence."

"That's why you asked for my password the last time you were here," I said reluctantly, reaching for my tablet. I'd been using it ever since the police asked for my laptop. I opened up the Twitter app. "Can I change my password now?"

Papa walked over to me. "All of that can be taken care of later." He grabbed my tablet. He walked back across the room to Officer Gray.

At this point, nothing else could surprise me. I'd been played by one of my father's friends, who wasn't that savvy on social media but found someone who was. Only she wasn't as smart as she thought she was and the very thing that they used to try to trap me was ultimately their own demise. I was glad they were locked up, but I didn't feel so happy.

"Bre, it's okay," Emé said, walking over to hug me. "It's over now."

I sighed. "No. It's not," I said. "At the end of the day, I'm the one they played. I'm the one who didn't see it coming. On top of all that, I'm the one in the hospital. Not to mention, Mama and Papa will probably put more restrictions on me than I had before." I was crying and sputtering, but I didn't care. I was on a rampage. "It seems I go forward six steps and get knocked back seven. I shut down my fitness classes because I *had* to. I started the online business because I *had* to. Papa set me up with in home care because he *had* to. Nothing for me will ever be the same. I'm not safe whether I have a gym located on Broad street or one in my own home."

I looked at Papa who was coming over to me. "How can you say it's over? We're the Clovers, right?"

This was the second time I'd ever despised my name since I'd been diagnosed. I guess that's what they meant when they said with every blessing comes a burden. I was just waiting for mine to lighten up.

❀ ❀ ❀

The rain belted fiercely against the window. It had been thundering and lightning for the last hour. I placed my head against the glass, squinting from the glare of headlights. I'd been standing like this, watching the rain fall ever since Mama made everyone get out and give me some breathing room. I only let Desmond stay. I looked over at him. He fell asleep reading the Bible to me. I looked back towards the window and closed my eyes.

"God, I know I shouldn't question you, but I am. Because I don't understand," I prayed. "I'm tired. I know you promised me rest if I trust you, but how? How can I trust you when everything looks so dark, right now?"

I wiped a tear from my eye. "I'm not asking you to heal me. I'm just asking for peace. It seems like I can't tap into it like I used to. Is it me? Am I the one that moved away from you?"

"No."

I turned around to see Desmond standing behind me. I broke down crying just as he grabbed me. "No. You didn't move, Bre. He just trusts you. That's all." He kissed my forehead. "You remember that sermon our Pastor preached about God being able to trust Abraham. That's why he asked him to offer his son Isaac. It was all a test to see if Abraham would be willing to give God the very thing he had asked God for."

I sobbed into his shoulder as he rubbed my back. "How does that apply to me? I didn't ask God for lupus."

"But you asked Him for strength."

I pulled away from him. "Huh?"

"He always gives his hardest battle to his strongest soldier. You're stronger than you think, kiddo."

I wiped at my face. "And you say that because..."

He gave my hair a gentle tug. "You always were the sarcastic one."

I smiled. "It's nice to be myself, even if it's just for a few minutes."

He nudged me, and I nudged him back. "I said it because you are. Our family unit is strong, but we've been going through some things. I'm sure you can see Dad and I having our moments. Emé and Mama. Cashmere and whichever guy she's dating for the month."

We shared a laugh.

"I think it's Robbie again," I joked.

"Whatever," he said. "All I'm saying is, we're the ones crying, breaking down every five minutes when you have an attack, or you say you're in pain. We sweat just thinking of a needle going into your arm for a life-threatening disease. But you? You stand up every time and take it."

"Are you crazy? Did you see me earlier? I had snot all over my face."

He wrapped me in a hug. "That you'd probably been holding in for the last what, eight months? I've seen you cry all of maybe six times, and two of those times were when I spanked you in basketball."

245

"Lies. That's a lie," I said, pinching him.

"Sis, I've never seen someone so patient when things don't go her way, so loving when times are calling her to be hateful and so peaceful when everything is screaming war. You are strong, Bre. When we prayed together as kids, you remember what you used to pray?"

I rolled my eyes in the air. "Yes. I do. God, I want to be strong like Papa. Make me strong. Then I'd flex, like this." I posed.

He laughed. "And you always tried to match him when he worked out. You wanted to lift what he lifted. You just knew you could handle it."

"I could."

He looked at me. It all sunk in what he was saying. "Yes. You can. You're not just physically strong because you love fitness and eat right. You're the strongest person I know. Even Papa cried during chemotherapy."

I popped his arm. "Shhh. Nobody is supposed to know that."

We stared at each other. There was a silence only we understood. I lifted my clover chain and held onto the charm. "Clover Strength?"

He reached for his and did the same. "God's strength. Clover Pride," he said, finishing.

We knew where our help came from. Mama and Papa never let us forget it; humility before honor. We hugged again.

"I love you, Des. Thanks for always being there," I said. "Oh and sorry your birthday got overlooked."

"I got to spend it with you," he said. "And I'll always be here. I love you more."

As we parted, we looked out the window together, my arm still around his waist and his around my shoulder. I shielded my eyes from another set of headlights that was pulling up at the hospital's entrance. It was a black Benz. I knew I couldn't have any visitors this late, but I had asked Saith to stop by. Myla and his father had an emergency, and he ended up canceling. I was hoping he would still try to make it, even though my visiting hours were long over. It's only nine. Maybe I can convince Papa to let him up. I saw a guy get out of the car and walk around to the passenger side. He opened the door. When I saw who was getting in, I gasped. Desmond's arms tightened around my shoulder.

"Damn it," he said.

"Where's Cashmere going?" I asked.

I knew he didn't know. I was pretty sure at that moment that nobody knew. She'd just told our parents earlier that she was going to get more focused. Now I realized it was easier to ask for forgiveness than to ask for permission. She said all the right things so that they wouldn't have to say them first. The smile I had on my face a moment ago was slowly fading. Not because I wasn't happy. My story was just beginning – and so was my family's drama. I had a feeling my parents would never be able to rest or take their end of the summer vacation. They would spend the rest of this summer and next, chasing Cashmere.

Mya Kay, born and raised in North Philadelphia, is a bestselling author, speaker and literary coach who believes everyone has a story to tell. She has been honing her craft since she first discovered her calling for writing and publishing ten years ago. She has published eleven books and is currently signed to The TMG Firm as an author. Visit www.writermya.com to keep up with her success.